The Moriah Confession

The Moriah Confession

Lee Nelson

Readers respond to Lee Nelson books

One night at the dinner table I was telling my mother about Lee Nelson's books. I picked up one of the books to show her some of the pictures. I thumbed through the pages a full five minutes before I realized there were no "real pictures," only the word pictures created in my mind.

David Noyes
Preston, Idaho

Lee Nelson and Louis L'Amour are the most popular authors in the Utah prison system.

Dennis Christensen
Librarian, Utah State Prison

Walkara, by Lee Nelson, is truly one of the most interesting, educational, and fascinating books I have read. Once I got into it, I simply didn't want to put it down until I had reached the final page at 3:30 a.m. this morning.

Judge Donald Nicholson
Corsicana, Texas

I am a teacher of 8th grade reading. Mr. Nelson's Storm Testament books are the most widely circulated books in our school library.

Janet Carroll
Hyde Park, Utah

Lee Nelson's books captivate me to the point where I do not want to put them down. It gives me much pleasure to sit down and get lost in one of these stories. My favorite authors are Shakespeare, Dumas, L'Amour, Twain, and now Lee Nelson.

Janet Howard
Hampstead, Maryland

My favorite Lee Nelson book is Storm Testament V. I have read this book at least a dozen times, and love it every time.

Ryan Stout
Colorado Springs, Colorado

Lee Nelson is the best western writer of them all. When I read one of his books, it puts me in the saddle right next to the main character all the way through the book. One of the marks of a good writer is the pain and suffering the reader goes through when the book is finished and there is nothing more to read. Lee Nelson does this.

Scott Morrison
Provo, Utah

Oh how much I enjoyed a borrowed copy of Walkara. I hate to give it back. I keep thumbing through it. I bought the rest of the Storm Testament series, thinking they would provide an entire winter of reading, but I found I could not leave them alone, and was finished long before the snow melted.

Elaine Freestone
Bountiful, Utah

We are most in the dark
when we are the most certain,
and the most enlightened
when we are the most confused.

M. Scott Peck

Prologue

Ella Tanner stepped out of her gold Jeep Cherokee and slammed the door. Too hard. It was Saturday, and the early morning sun in a clear Utah sky was still hidden behind Loafer Peak east of Spanish Fork. The maples, aspen and oaks were just beginning to show their fall colors.

She was parked at the bottom of Bishop Jensen's asparagus field where Sister Jensen said he was taking a water turn. The previous evening Ella had decided to talk to her bishop on Sunday, but after another sleepless night, she could wait no longer.

A lifetime of religious training, and the accompanying convictions, could not be ignored. She had tried. She wanted desperately to protect her secret from what she thought would be the uncaring scrutiny of those who could never understand. But all her life she had been taught that serious transgressions of God's law, including adultery, especially adultery, must be confessed.

Ella had also been taught that in addition to confession, true repentance was accompanied by a godly sorrow for the sin committed. She wasn't exactly sure what godly sorrow

1

was, only that she was not experiencing it. At least she didn't think she was.

Earlier, she had convinced herself that without deep remorse for her sin, confession would be a waste of time. But the sleepless nights, and the dull, aching sob in her chest, would not go away. Ella knew something inside her was terribly amiss. Sometimes she felt if something didn't happen soon, she might die. Perhaps the act of confession would begin some kind of healing process.

She could see Bishop Jensen at the head of the asparagus patch. He was busy with his shovel, and hadn't seen her yet. She started towards him.

Ella had turned 37 during the summer, but people often thought she was much younger. While shopping at the mall or jogging at the Brigham Young University track with her daughter, Laura, people often thought the two were sisters. Both shared the same long, blond hair, with loosely cropped bangs extending below the eyebrows. But Ella's eyes were more blue in color, her cheekbones more pronounced, and her jaw more square. During her mid-twenties, Ella had modeled sleep wear and undergarments in print advertisements for the ZCMI department store chain.

Ella found herself the subject of frequent flirtations by returned missionaries in the English classes she taught at BYU, where she was an assistant professor of English. Such flirtations always ended when the young men saw the silver ring on her wedding finger and found out she was the mother of two teenage children.

But all that was irrelevant now. She had serious business with the bishop. He could see her as she marched towards him through the waist-high asparagus plants.

Ella was wearing faded Wrangler jeans, white sneakers without stockings, and a peach-colored T-shirt—attire that flattered her well-maintained figure, but hardly appropriate garb for the serious business of confession.

Bishop Jensen wasn't dressed for the occasion either,

wearing knee-high rubber boots, soiled Levis and a short-sleeved blue and white western shirt with snap-down flaps over the pockets. The front of his shirt was tight over a well-rounded paunch, used to too much mashed potatoes and gravy—but he was not too fat, at least not for an aging biology professor. He was in his mid-sixties, with thinning gray hair around the sides of his otherwise bald head. He did not wear the usual ball cap worn by most farmers.

Ella was glad her bishop was not one of those young ones she had known over the years, caught up in the self-importance of being called to a major church position at an early age. She felt good bishops, like good writers, needed the seasoning and wisdom that come only with age and experience.

"Good morning, Sister Tanner," Jensen called, when she was close enough to hear his voice. "Where's your shovel?"

"Wore it out trying to dig a hole to crawl into," she called back, surprised at her cheerful spontaneity.

"Thought maybe you wanted to borrow my keys to the church," he said, more serious. She was close now.

"You may not want me in the church when you hear what I have to say," Ella said, wanting to get to the point, having no desire to tiptoe around the edges of the matter with small talk.

"Whoa," the bishop said, trying to slow her down, sensing her intensity. "Maybe this should wait until tomorrow, in my office at the church."

"I feel perfectly at home in an asparagus patch, if you do," she said. "I'd rather not wait. Is that all right?"

The bishop placed his rubber boot on the business end of his shovel and pushed the steel spade into the muddy soil.

"Let's go over to the ditch bank," he said. "There's a comfortable spot under the walnut tree."

"I don't know if that's necessary," she said nervously. "What I have to say, won't take very long."

"Come," he said, starting to walk towards the tree. Reluctantly, she followed.

The bishop seated himself on the ground, his back against the rough bark of the trunk. Ella straddled a fallen log, about five feet from the tree. She was not facing the bishop, at least not directly. That pleased her.

Bishop Jensen picked a piece of orchard grass and thoughtfully pushed one end into his mouth. He seemed relaxed, and in no hurry to get started. Ella guessed he had listened to many confessions, and was used to this kind of thing. She was not.

"All my life I have been taught that serious sins must be confessed to the proper church authority," she said. The bishop nodded, but no words came from his mouth, which still held the piece of grass.

"I have committed adultery," she said, the words coming easier than she had thought they would. Ella stopped, feeling somewhat relieved that she had finally confessed, but also feeling awkward. The bishop said nothing. Nor did he look surprised or shocked. He continued to play with the piece of grass.

"Now that you have my confession, guess I'll be heading home," she said, starting to get up.

"Hold your horses, sister," he said, his voice warm but firm. He motioned for her to sit back down. "We're not through, not by a long shot."

"But I gave you my confession," she protested, reluctantly returning to her seat on the log.

"That's not enough," Jensen said quietly. "I need the whole story."

"Do you want a pornographic description?" she asked, sarcasm in her voice. The bishop didn't answer her question.

"As your bishop, I am your judge in Israel," he said. "How can I judge you if I don't know what happened?"

"I said I committed adultery. That should be enough."

"It isn't," he said. "If you are confessing to being

4

molested by an uncle when you were twelve years old, I would judge you differently than if you had sex with five members of the BYU football team last night. How can I judge you, and help you, if I don't know the whole story?''

"Before I tell you anything else," she said cautiously, "can I assume this interview is confidential?"

"All my interviews are confidential."

"You will tell no one?"

"I won't announce it in Sunday school," he said.

"Then you will tell no one," she probed.

"There will probably be a bishop's court. My two counselors will have to know. Also the ward clerk."

Ella shuddered. The wives of these men were her friends, two of them good friends. She doubted all four of the men involved in her court could keep their mouths shut.

"No one else?" she asked.

"If the man you are or were involved with is a member of the Church I will probably call his bishop or stake president so he will have an opportunity to clear this up."

"No one else?"

"If there is anything difficult or unusual, I will probably discuss it with our stake president."

"No one else will know?"

"You work for BYU, the Church university. Your administrative superiors and the appropriate general authorities will have to know."

By this time Ella had lost count of all the people who were going to be told about her confidential confession.

"I am an English professor," she said, a hint of anger in her voice. "Using the word confidential to describe this interview is a blatant misuse of the language."

"Like I said, I am not going to tell your story in Sunday school," the bishop responded deliberately. "I am not going to talk about it at the barber shop or over the back fence, nor am I going to send a news release to the *Daily Herald*. But for administrative reasons, the appropriate church and university leaders will have to be notified."

"For the first time in my life I regret not being a Catholic," Ella said. There was a look of surprise on the bishop's face.

"Catholic priests know what confidential means," she continued. "They don't tell anyone what they hear in confession. I wish I were a Catholic today."

"I can see you are upset," the bishop said. "Would you rather continue this some other time, perhaps tomorrow in my office?"

"No. If you give me time to think about this confidentiality thing, I'll never get my confession out. If it's got to be done, I might as well do it now. Where should I start?"

"With whom did you commit adultery?" he asked.

"I am not ready to tell you that, at least not yet," she said.

"Is it someone I know?" he asked.

"No. I don't think so. Let's start somewhere else."

"Where did it happen?" he asked.

"Mt. Moriah."

"That sounds like a name from a song, not a real place," he said.

"It is a real place, a very real place," Ella said. "It's a beautiful mountain, on the Nevada-Utah border—a pristine wilderness with golden eagles, bighorn sheep, lots of deer and wild horses, and some spectacular scenery. But that's not all."

"Please continue," the bishop urged.

"The trees," she said. "They are the oldest living things on the face of the earth. Some of them are nearly three thousand years old. Bristlecone pines. The little cones are bluer than the Pacific Ocean on a clear day. When you walk among them you feel like you are in God's own garden. It's a holy place."

"So you went there to commit adultery?"

Prologue

"I can see this isn't going to work," Ella said, starting to get up.

"I'm sorry I said that," Jensen responded. "I was insensitive. Please sit down. I am ready to hear the Moriah confession."

"What did you say?"

"I am ready to hear the Moriah confession."

"I like what you call it."

"Then tell me the rest."

"OK."

Chapter 1

Ella left Spanish Fork at five in the morning. Three hours later she had been on dirt roads for 50 miles, and hadn't seen a house in a hundred miles. She was approaching Trout Creek, Utah, near the Nevada border, about 90 miles south of Wendover.

She hadn't seen a gas station in 100 miles, either, and hoped there would be one here. If not, she had made a big mistake not bringing along a five-gallon can with extra fuel.

To the left, about a hundred yards east of the road, behind some corrals and haystacks, Ella saw an old white house with smoke coming from the chimney. Freshly painted letters on the mailbox said Thousand Peaks Ranch. Finally, she had reached a place where people lived. She felt better.

To her amazement, the next building was a brand-new Mormon church, not as big as the ones in populated areas, but neat and clean with a freshly cut lawn. It was the first church she had ever seen with cattle guards to keep livestock out of the churchyard. There were enough parking places for about 30 cars. Ella wondered where the people lived who went to church here. Probably just around the corner, where she hoped to find fuel.

As Ella continued down the road, she found no gas station, only a huge lot full of abandoned farm equipment. Beyond the equipment to the east was a cinder-block house with smoke coming from the chimney. Farther up the road was nothing, only seemingly endless groves of wild Russian olive trees. So much for Trout Creek. A town with two dwellings hardly justified a gas station. Not even a pay phone or a Coke machine. The big surprise was the new church.

Ella stopped her Jeep Cherokee and opened her Utah Atlas. She had filled her tank in Nephi during the pre-dawn hours. Now she had a little less than half a tank of fuel, not enough to get back to Nephi, but enough to get to Delta, which she guessed was about a hundred miles away.

As she looked over the map, she wondered if there would be gas in Ibapah, which she thought was about ten miles due west on the other side of the snow-covered Deep Creek Mountains. But there was no road going over the mountains. She could get to Ibapah going around the mountains to the north, or around the south end. Either way the distance would be about 50 miles, she guessed.

Ella was not on a pleasure jaunt, nor was there anyone in particular she wanted to visit in this desolate section of Utah's west desert. She was doing research for an article she hoped to publish on a long-forgotten battle between the United States Army and a huge band of Indians, mostly Goshutes, that took place around 1860, somewhere near the south end of the Deep Creek Mountains, probably in a place called Pleasant Valley.

The fact that a battle in which over 300 Indians died was not highly publicized, not even at the time it happened, led Ella to suspect that instead of a great battle, there had been a great slaughter of women and children, statistics that looked impressive on military reports but could not bear the scrutiny of objective investigation. Maybe she could be the one to finally, after 135 years, bring the true story to light.

Chapter 1

At the university, teachers were encouraged to do original research and to publish. Some in the administration and faculty fondly referred to Brigham Young University as the Harvard of the West as they demanded higher standards in research and teaching.

While all this was good, she had her doubts the school could ever reach the highest levels of academic excellence when it was owned and controlled by a church which frowned on faculty and student criticism of its doctrines, administrative policies, and leaders.

Still, Ella was glad for the pressure to publish. Without it, she would probably be content to just teach. She had to admit that over the years her research and writing projects, though difficult, had been rewarding. Every year she tried to pick out a little-known piece of history to research and write about.

She had learned about the Goshute massacre from a retired schoolteacher, Dan Roberts, whom she had met at a meeting of the Utah Historical Society. He had told her about his efforts to locate the battle site in Pleasant Valley. Later, she had found a description of the battle and the events leading up to it, written by Elijah "Nick" Wilson, who had been a guide for the Army at the time of the massacre. She had corresponded with the Department of Defense in Washington, and had received several copies of obscure documents relating to General Albert Sidney Johnston's military campaigns in Utah.

Now she was coming to the location. Ella wanted to study the geography and compare what she found with Wilson's account. She wanted to hike around the apparent battle location, and get the feel of the place. She wanted to talk to people, whites and Indians. Maybe she would find some things that Dan Roberts didn't know. In fact, she had a hunch she was about to make an important historical discovery, and she had learned over the years not to ignore such hunches.

Ella was glad to be spending a spring day in the west

11

desert. Especially, she was glad to be away from home, where her husband, George, was totally involved in the upcoming spring football scrimmage.

George worked in the athletic department at BYU, where his whole life was consumed with the success and failure of the BYU football and basketball teams. He worshipped the coaches, and idolized the players. Not only did he know all of them by name, but he knew how many touchdowns or tackles they had made in high school, how much weight they could bench press, and how fast they could run the 40-yard dash. George went to every home game, watched as many as possible on television, and listened to the rest on the radio. Ella didn't think George had ever missed the rebroadcast of a big game. She guessed George had seen the BYU-Miami football game at least 10 times. When BYU was winning, George was happy. When BYU lost, George was miserable, and his misery continued until the next victory. While BYU teams won most of the time, it seemed the season usually ended with a loss, which extended George's period of mourning long into the off-season.

Ella felt sorry for George for being so wrapped up in something twice removed from the real world. The first level of insulation was the fact that football and basketball were only games where men and women moved balls across lines or through metal hoops. Ella failed to understand how a game could be so important to so many people. Ella wished George could do something useful, like open a group home for troubled teenagers or even build a garage so he could stand back and think that long after he was dead people would still be using that garage.

The second level of insulation from the real world was the fact that poor George was only a spectator to the games he loved. He never caught a pass or fumbled when the score was tied. He didn't even play catch with his own boy. He was totally occupied with watching other people do it.

George's only real contribution to the game of football was the time he smeared Crisco on the goalposts before a game with the University of Utah. When the game was over the students couldn't tear the goalposts down because they couldn't climb the poles. George was given a plaque at the annual sports banquet—an award for the man who had saved the goalposts. People were clapping and whistling as if he had saved the box turtles. For the next few years, some of the players fondly called George the Crisco Kid.

She remembered when she had dated George in college. He had seemed ambitious and intense in his studies, and she had believed he would find success in the business world. He had been an avid sports fan at the time, but Ella thought his priorities would change once he became a husband and father. She was wrong. His passion for sports only grew, as did his girth as he spent countless hours in front of the television watching sporting events, a bowl of popcorn in one hand and a pitcher of Kool-Aid in the other.

Ella had tried to be a supportive wife. She attended many of the games. Then one day she realized both of her children were conceived during the off-season. George loved football more than her. She decided to have her own life, apart from BYU sports. George could save the goalposts by himself.

Ella closed the map book and started her engine. She decided to go to Pleasant Valley and hike the area where Roberts said the massacre had taken place. Black squares on the map indicated there were two houses in the area. If anyone still lived there she would talk to them. Then she would continue around the southern end of the mountains to Ibapah, where she could get gas. If there was a motel, she would spend the night. If not, she would continue north to Wendover. Hopefully, some of the Indians in Ibapah would talk to her.

It was probably her thoughts about George and his sports that caused the extra surge of adrenaline in her veins. She pressed on the gas pedal with too much enthusiasm, driving too fast down a lane crowded on both sides with willows and wild olive trees.

Suddenly, four deer scampered to get out of the way. She hit the brakes, too late. The Jeep hit the last deer.

The thump didn't seem very hard or jarring, but the deer went down as the Jeep slid to a halt. Ella clung to the steering wheel for a few seconds to get her emotions under control, then jumped out to survey the damage.

The right side of the bumper was slightly bent, and the headlight above it was broken. Otherwise the Jeep seemed all right. But not the deer. The young buck was on the ground, terror in his big, soft eyes. He was kicking aimlessly at the air with one of his hind legs.

Ella didn't know what to do. She sensed the deer ought to be put out of his misery, but she did not have a gun, and even if she had one, she didn't know if she could pull the trigger to end the life of a helpless animal.

It occurred to her she might be able to kill the deer by running over it with the Jeep. But if she tried that, maybe she would just push it along the road, causing the helpless animal even more pain and suffering without killing it. No, the best thing to do would be to go back to one of the houses and find someone to help. The people who lived in the area would know what to do. Ella turned to get into the Jeep, then stopped.

A man on a horse was riding towards her. Apparently, he had ridden up while she had been looking at the deer. He looked a young like Tommy Lee Jones in cowboy clothes, right off the movie set. He wore a weathered, black cowboy hat, low in the front and back. The band was thin, with red and black colors creating some kind of Indian design.

His eyes were gray and fierce like those of a wolf. The skin on his face had a deep tan from frequent exposure to sun and wind. His whiskers hadn't been shaved in several days, but that only added to the rugged masculinity of the man. His shoulders were broad, his arms muscular, his stomach as flat as a spatula, a rare quality in the grown men Ella knew.

The cowboy wore a red bandanna, a gray cotton shirt with long sleeves, and faded Wrangler jeans. He wore short

14

chaps, the kind that go only to the knees. His scuffed boots carried large silver spurs.

"Deer season doesn't open 'til October," he said in a friendly drawl as he pulled his horse to a halt. The animal was sorrel in color, with a white star in the middle of its forehead. It had the well-muscled look of the calf roping and bulldogging horses she had seen on television.

"There were three more," Ella said. "Guess I'm lucky I hit only one."

With the grace of a gymnast, the stranger stepped out of the saddle. He handed her one of the reins, while reaching for a knife in a leather pouch attached to his belt.

"Maybe we should call a veterinarian," Ella suggested, realizing afterwards that it was a dumb thing to say. She just was not ready to see the animal die.

"Looks like a broken back," the stranger said. "Not even a vet can fix that. Need to put the poor fellow out of his misery." Opening the knife blade, he stepped forward. Ella did not look away.

Moving behind the deer, the stranger grabbed an ear with his left hand so he could hold the head steady, then he began cutting its throat with the knife. First, he sliced the artery on one side, then the other. By the time he pulled his hand away, it was covered with blood. The deer stopped kicking. The frightened look faded from its eyes as the blood oozed and squirted onto the new grass.

"What do you want to do with it?" the cowboy asked, turning towards Ella.

"I think you are supposed to call the fish and game office," she offered. "They send out a game warden, who takes it to an orphanage or homeless shelter."

"The nearest fish and game office is two hundred miles away in Springville," he countered. "The meat would probably spoil by the time anyone came, but I don't think they would come this far."

"Do you want it?" she asked. "We shouldn't let it go to waste."

"I don't need it. Lots of beef in the freezer. But I know someone who would. We can take it up to Bruce."

"Who?"

"Bruce, a hermit who lives in an old mining shack where Trout Creek runs out of the mountain," he explained, nodding west towards the high mountains.

"All by himself? What does he do?"

"Hunts a few rabbits, keeps a tidy cabin. Smokes a little pot. Every few years the sheriff drives up there and pulls up his marijuana plants."

"Where's he from?"

"Some say he's a shell-shocked Vietnam vet. Others say he escaped from a California prison. Don't think he gets a welfare check. Doesn't hurt anyone. I take him supplies once in a while—beans, rice, coffee, some .22 shells. He watches our cows that run in a pasture up there in the summer. We call it the bobcat pasture."

"Would I be able to find it by myself?" Ella asked.

"One wrong turn and you'd never find the place. I should go with you. But first I better gut this thing out." Quickly he bent over the deer, cut open the skin on the soft underbelly and began removing the entrails. When he was finished, he carefully lifted the deer into the back of the Jeep. While he was doing this, Ella tied the horse to the nearest fence post.

When she returned to the Jeep she noticed the pile of entrails beside the road.

"What should we do with this?" she asked.

"Leave it. What else?" the stranger asked, obviously surprised by her comment.

"We shouldn't litter."

"Excuse me," he said. "Leaving a gut pile on the side of the road is not littering."

"I am a professor of English, and I can't think of a better word."

"I know a better word," he said, not backing down. "Recycling."

16

Chapter 1

"Can you defend your choice?" she asked, confident a cowboy could not match wits with an English professor in a word game.

"Sure," he said. "Tonight a couple of coyotes will come along and slick up this stuff. When they're done, they'll go over in the grass and do their business. Where they do it the grass will grow greener and taller. A young buck will come along and eat up that greener, taller grass. When his belly is full, he'll look across the road at a couple of good-looking does and decide he wants to pay a visit. When he starts to run over there, a lady from Spanish Fork runs into him and kills him. Bingo, the recycle is complete."

Ella was both surprised and impressed with the cowboy's ability to express himself.

"Before you get in my car I want to know your name," she said.

"Emmett. Emmett Hays," he said. "Pleased to meet you. Wish we could have met under more favorable circumstances."

"My name is Ella Tanner," she said. "How did you know I was from Spanish Fork?"

"Did I say you were from Spanish Fork?"

"Yes, during the recycling speech."

"If I said it, it was an accident. I just met you. You didn't say where you were from."

"A strange accident," she mused. "Anyway, I'm glad to meet you, Mr. Emmett Hays." Ella reached out to shake hands, but when he held out his hand, she quickly withdrew hers. His hand was still covered with the blood of the deer.

"Mr. Hays," she said, "I can see you are not one of the spectators of the world."

There was silence between them as Emmett reached into his pocket, removed a handkerchief and began to wipe the blood from his hands.

"I don't know what you mean," he began thoughtfully, "but I think you are correct in assuming a man with blood on his hands is not one of the spectators of the world."

17

The Moriah Confession

A minute later they were headed back up the road, hauling a dead deer to the bobcat hermit.

Chapter 2

The road to the bobcat pasture was rough. At times it seemed to Ella they were just driving over rocks and sagebrush, on no road at all. But after winding their way through a grove of pinion pine and juniper trees, the hermit's cabin suddenly appeared in front of them.

In her travels along the back roads of Utah, Ella had seen many old cabins. This one was larger than most, and in remarkably good condition. Dirt was on the roof.

Emmett didn't waste any time getting out and checking the front door to see if Bruce was home. Ella stepped out of the Jeep and soaked in the magnificent view of Snake Valley to the east, and beyond the valley, the Confusion, Fish Springs and House Mountains—desert mountains looking forbidding and mysterious in the blue-gray haze of a cool spring morning. She regretted the position of the late morning sun, preventing her from capturing the breathtaking view on film.

"He's not home," Emmett called from the open doorway.

"I guessed that, when there was no car or truck parked outside," she responded, without thinking.

"Bruce doesn't have a car or truck," Emmett shot back. "He's a hermit, remember?"

"How far are we from the nearest grocery store?" Ella asked, wondering how anyone could live this far away from anything, without a car or truck."

"Maybe a hundred miles," Emmett said. "But there's a gas station about 50 miles to the south, on Highway 50."

"He doesn't have a bike or a horse either?" she asked.

"Nope. But he's got a deer, now. Plenty to eat for a while."

"Then where is he?" she wanted to know.

"Could have walked down to the valley. Maybe he's just off in the hills, hunting."

"How does he get things, like groceries, books, medicine?" she asked, feeling stupid but curious.

"I bring him a box of groceries once in a while—rice, beans, coffee, stuff like that. Sometimes bullets and tobacco. People in the valley give him things, too."

"That's very kind of you," she said sincerely.

"Not really. Bruce watches our cows when they are up here. He has helped us brand a few times. The least I can do is bring him a little food once in a while."

Ella helped Emmett lift the deer out of the back of the Jeep and carry it through the front door of the cabin. They placed it on the floor.

Ella looked around. There was a wood stove by the door, and next to it a wooden box containing some freshly split pieces of pinion pine. Across from the stove was a plank table. On it was a dinner plate and a tin cup containing several forks and spoons. Beyond the table was a cot with a neatly-folded army blanket on it. That was all. No pictures on the walls. No extra jackets on pegs by the door. No boots lying about. No books or magazines.

Chapter 2

"This is more austere than a jail cell," she said. "Why would anyone want to live this way?"

"Beats me. You ought to come back when Bruce is home and ask him."

"I would like that. What's he like?"

"Quiet, polite. Looks at you when he talks to you. Last time I was up here, he offered me a plate of spaghetti."

"You ate it?"

"Of course. It was lunchtime. Actually, it was pretty good. The sauce had mushrooms in it. Don't know how a man would get mushrooms up here."

"You didn't ask?"

"Figure a man has a reason to live alone like this. Maybe he likes his privacy. Maybe he doesn't like too many questions. As it is, he watches my cows and I bring him food. That's all there is between me and Bruce. Ought to have more relationships like this. Keeps life from getting too complicated."

"Do you really mean that?" Ella asked, as they returned to the Jeep. He didn't answer as they climbed inside and started back down the mountain. It wasn't until they were leaving the pinion and juniper grove that he spoke.

"When things go wrong it's easier to walk away from the shallow relationships," he said thoughtfully.

"Don't you mean if, instead of when, things go wrong?" she asked.

"I think this conversation is getting too personal, too philosophical, and too boring," he said. "Tell me what brings you to this practically uninhabited wasteland."

Ella told him about her research project, and how she hoped to visit Pleasant Valley where the schoolteacher, Dan Roberts, said the Goshute massacre had taken place.

"That's where I live," Emmett said. "I can show you where Roberts dug some holes. I think he was trying to find some artifacts left over from the battle."

"You know where the battle took place?" she asked.

"I didn't say that. I said I know where Roberts dug

21

some holes.''

"Could Roberts be wrong?''

"If you read the Nick Wilson account in *White Indian Boy*, he mentions a lake below the battle site. There's no lake in Pleasant Valley. But there are plenty of springs and flat bottom lands. There could have been a lake at one time, before the first farmers ran the water off in ditches.''

"Why does Roberts think the battle was in Pleasant Valley?''

"Wilson was a scout for the Army. He said the battle took place at the south end of the Deep Creek Mountains in a canyon above one of Brigham Young's old mail stations. Brigham Young had a mail station where my house is in Pleasant Valley, and that's at the south end of the Deep Creek Mountains. The only problem is the alleged lake or pond.''

"I'm surprised to find a cowboy so well-versed in history,'' Ella said, meaning to pay Emmett a compliment.

"Why's that?'' he asked abruptly.

"I just have a hard time seeing a cowboy sitting at a desk reading a history book.''

"What do you think we do on long winter nights? We don't have television reception out here.''

"You don't go to saloons to drink, pick up girls, ride mechanical bulls, then drive your pickup truck up and down Main Street when you don't have tickets to a George Strait performance?''

"Who's George Strait?''

"You've got to be kidding,'' she said, genuinely surprised. "You really don't know who George Strait is?''

"Has he been to the NFR, the national finals rodeo?''

"I'm sure he goes every year.''

"What event?''

"You can't be serious.''

"I am.''

"George Strait doesn't have an event. He's a singer, one of the most popular country singers of all time.''

"Then he's not a real cowboy.''

Chapter 2

"It really surprises me to find a cowboy who is not part of the country-western culture."

"I don't know if you should assume that much. I'm familiar with the art work of Gary Erickson, the poetry of Baxter Black and Waddie Mitchell, even the sculpting of Jeff Wolf. Bet you don't know who he is. Rode bulls for eight years. Grew up in Goshen, right by Spanish Fork."

"None of the people you mention are in the same class with George Strait," she argued.

"But they're all cowboys."

"So is George. He's what you call a team roper. He catches the feet."

"OK, Mrs. Smarty Pants," Emmett countered. "I'll agree this George Strait is an important cowboy singer, and that an English professor from Spanish Fork wrote the cowboy Book of Knowledge, if you'll answer just one question."

"Go ahead, ask it," she challenged. Ella was surprised at her feelings, how much she was enjoying this unusual interchange with this backwoods cowboy from Pleasant Valley, a place probably no one on the entire BYU faculty had ever heard of.

"Who are Jake Barnes and Clay O'Brien Cooper?" he asked.

"I don't know," she answered.

"Then who is Michael Jordan?" There was an unmistakable note of sarcasm in his voice.

"Everybody knows who Michael Jordan is," she said. "He's certainly not a cowboy."

"How many times did he lead the Chicago Bulls to world championships?" he asked.

"I don't know, maybe two or three times."

"Maybe two or three times," he said, mimicking her. "And people say he's the greatest athlete ever to play sports."

"I don't know why you are talking about Michael Jordan," she complained. "You are starting to sound like my husband."

"Jake Barnes and Clay O'Brien Cooper have won the

world championship of team roping seven times," he said, not to be distracted by Ella's comment about her husband. "There are 600 players in the NBA who competed with Michael Jordan in basketball, but there are fifty thousand team ropers who would like a shot at the world championship, and Jake and Clay have won it seven times. It's amazing. No cowboy in history has ever come close to winning the world championship of any event seven times. If Jake and Clay were standing in the road in front of us, I would get out of the Jeep, crawl up to them on my hands and knees and kiss their boots."

"You would not," Ella challenged.

"I would feel like doing it."

"I think this conversation is getting too personal, too philosophical, and too boring," she said.

"You don't want to talk about Jake and Clay, the two greatest ropers of all time?"

"I don't want to talk about sports."

"Then what do you want to discuss?"

"How about you, Emmett Hays, the cowboy with bloody hands who has been riding in my Jeep for an hour. All I know about you is that you enjoy shallow relationships. I hope there's more. Tell me."

"What do you want to know?"

"For starters, is there a female in your life?"

"Several, you might even say many," he said bluntly.

Ella gasped, unthinkingly removing one hand from the steering wheel and placing it over her mouth. She had read about the many groups of Mormon fundamentalists, or polygamists, who had moved to the remote areas of Utah to escape the mainstream of society. Was this handsome cowboy one of them? She had heard of the Allreds, the Jessops, and the LeBarons—but she couldn't connect the Hays name with polygamy.

"Would you mind explaining what you mean by many?" she asked carefully.

"About three hundred," he said matter-of-factly.

Chapter 2

"King Solomon didn't have that many wives," she responded quickly, beginning to believe she had actually picked up a real polygamist.

"Who said anything about wives?" he laughed. "I'm talking about mother cows. I have 300 bovine females who depend on me for their nourishment, safety and general happiness. They are the females in my life."

"You're not married?"

"Nope."

"Have you ever been married?"

"I think this conversation is getting too personal, too philosophical, and too boring," he said. They both laughed, though she did not agree with him. Conversation with Emmett Hays was anything but boring. He was a rational, intelligent human being with a healthy sense of humor. She had not been able to anticipate a single word he had said.

They were on the main road now. In front of them, Ella could see Emmett's horse tied to the fence, next to the pile of deer entrails. She knew when they reached the horse, she would have to stop the Jeep. He would get out, untie the horse, and step into the saddle. Or would he swing into the saddle like an Indian? She could not anticipate what Emmett Hays would do. Then he would ride away, or she would drive away, and she would never see him again. She didn't want to say goodby to Emmett Hays. Her hands tightened on the steering wheel as she slowly moved her foot from the gas pedal to the brake.

"Do you know how to ride a horse?" Emmett asked, his voice softer, less confident.

"I'm not a barrel racer," Ella said lightly, trying to cover up what was happening deep inside.

"My truck and trailer are up the road a piece," he explained, his voice even softer, almost like that of a child. "If you would like to follow me to the house, I'll saddle another horse and take you to the place where Roberts was digging."

"I would like that very much," she answered calmly,

fighting to hold down the overwhelming sense of relief and happiness that filled her entire being.

"I would like that very much," Ella said again, not realizing she was repeating herself, wondering if she was blushing with delight but not daring to look into the mirror to find out.

Chapter 3

Upon entering Pleasant Valley, following Emmett's truck and trailer, Ella's first reaction was to wonder why the place was called Pleasant Valley. The treeless hills on both sides of the road looked barren and brown, even in spring.

But gradually the scenery started to change. The Kern Mountains on the left began to look more like mountains than foothills. Beyond the barren hills on the right she started seeing the snow-capped peaks of the Deep Creek Range. In the valley bottoms, springs began to appear, then irrigated meadows. On the left she saw a wide, sweeping bed of purple wildflowers, the likes of which she had never seen before. Had she not been following Emmett she would have stopped to look more closely at them, and perhaps collected a sample for identification purposes.

When she saw the sign announcing she was entering Nevada, Ella could see junipers and pinion in the foothills leading to the now ruggedly majestic Kern Mountains. Cattle and horses were grazing in the meadows on her right. Then

Emmett turned right, at the end of a four-rail fence, into his driveway.

With wood siding and green trim, the house looked more like a chalet than a regular house. Several skylight windows on the east side caught the morning sun.

A short distance from the house was what appeared to be a bunkhouse. It was rectangular in shape with rustic siding, a green steel roof, and lots of windows with white trim. Ella could hardly wait to look inside.

Beyond the bunkhouse was a deep-blue kidney-shaped pond with several large boulders on one side, and a lone pine tree on the other. Beyond the pond were working corrals and a riding arena.

In the opposite direction from the house were several ancient log structures, a granary, several gas tanks, and a corral containing four or five horses.

Ella tried to understand the surge of excitement that was welling up inside her. While the mountain scenery was pleasant and beautiful, this was no Jackson Hole. While the buildings and improvements were more than adequate, they probably weren't rustic enough to be used as background for filming a western movie. No, the excitement she felt was not for the place, but for the man who lived here. How foolish, she thought. She still didn't know Emmett Hays. Perhaps he was a retired drug dealer or casino owner. Maybe he was an IRS agent on vacation, or a Mafia *patron* hiding from the FBI. She realized she needed to be more determined in schooling her feelings.

"What do you call this place?" Ella asked, after she got out of the Jeep. Emmett was leading Geronimo out of the trailer.

"Medicine Springs Ranch," he said quietly. "Lots of springs here. Indians, mostly Goshutes, used to camp here a lot, for hundreds of years. There are carvings on some of the rocks. I think it might have been a holy place."

"What do you mean?" she asked. "Did they do the bear dance here?"

28

Chapter 3

"I don't know what they did here," he said. "But one time when I walked out into the meadow with an old Indian, he said he felt a healing spirit. With tears in his eyes, he said this was a healing place, not only for the body, but for the spirit as well.

"Sometimes in the evening," Emmett continued, "just before dark, I walk out into the meadow. I look up at the mountains, listen to the stream, feel the soft soil under my feet, and wait. Sometimes I can feel what the Indian was talking about—like wounds, deep wounds, are finally beginning to heal."

"That's beautiful," she said.

"I don't know if beautiful is the best word to describe it, but it's real, at least it is for me. Excuse me while I go catch a horse for you."

He turned and walked towards the nearest gate, while Ella wondered what kind of hurt this man had endured, what kinds of wounds he carried, that he needed a healing place.

When Emmett returned to the gate, he was leading a sorrel mare, similar in appearance to Geronimo, but with more of a blaze on her forehead.

"She's beautiful," Ella said sincerely. "You really don't mind if I ride her?"

"No, and she won't mind either. She likes to get out for a ride." He began to brush the mare in preparation for putting on the blanket and saddle.

"What's her name?" Ella asked.

"Tithing," he said.

"Wait a minute," she said. "Nobody names a horse Tithing. That's no kind of name for a horse, a dog or anything else."

"Oh," Emmett said calmly, as he placed the blanket and saddle on the horse's back and began to put the latigo in the cinch ring.

"Why Tithing?" she asked.

"I have my reasons," he responded thoughtfully. "While they may not be philosophical or boring, they are

29

personal. I would rather not discuss them with a strange woman."

"You don't need to call me a strange woman," Ella scolded, grinning. "We kill and clean a deer together. You ride in my car while we do compassionate service to the poor, then I follow you like a lamb to the slaughter up fifteen miles of rough dirt road. Then you have the nerve to call me a strange woman."

"Any beautiful lady whom I have just met is a strange woman," he said, looking directly into her eyes.

Ella didn't know what to say, but she felt a blush coming on, one she couldn't hide. For the first time she felt like maybe it was time to get in her Jeep and drive away. But she didn't. It occurred to her that maybe he was trying to scare her away.

"Just tell me one thing," she said, gathering her wits. "Are you a Mormon?" She wanted to know if he was playing by the same rules that governed her life.

"Why do you want to know that?" he asked.

"Just curious," she said. "I mean, you live in Utah and have a horse named Tithing. I assume you are probably LDS."

"Actually, I live in Nevada. No, I am not a member of your church," he said. "But before I scare you off, let's get on the horses and ride to the massacre site."

Ella took a deep breath, fought back the urge to flee, and climbed on the horse. The stirrups were too long. When Emmett stepped beside her to make the necessary adjustments, his hand accidentally brushed against her leg.

An hour later they were riding high in the foothills above the ranch house, near a long valley extending down from the high mountains, which Emmett called Water Canyon. He led Ella through several meadows which he said were good camping places for Indians. He showed her several places where he thought Roberts had been digging. He also showed her an ancient rock with a weathered drawing of a bighorn sheep on it.

Chapter 3

Ella was relieved when Emmett finally suggested they tie the horses to a juniper tree and climb to the top of a rocky knoll. Ella wasn't used to riding. Her legs were getting sore, and her back was beginning to ache. She was ready for a break.

There was a shallow excavation at the top of the knoll, but Emmett assured her this was not a Roberts dig, but the work of a prospector looking for gold and silver. They sat on the rocky ground, a comfortable space between them, looking back over the gently sloping foothills.

"Tell me everything you know about the massacre," Ella said.

Thoughtfully, Emmett picked a piece of brush and put it in his mouth. "White sage," he said. "Thirty-five percent protein. Better for cows than grass, at least in winter."

"What about the massacre?" she asked, trying to get back on the subject that had brought them here.

"Just gathering my thoughts, lady," he said.

"I prefer not to be called lady," she protested.

"Do you hate that worse than being called a strange woman?"

"What about the massacre?" she asked.

"It was 1862, near the beginning of the Civil War," Emmett began. The words came easily, like he was a seasoned history lecturer at a large college.

"General Albert Sidney Johnston was stationed at Camp Floyd, west of Salt Lake City, with several companies of soldiers. Johnston was the officer who marched into Utah in 1858 and unseated Brigham Young as territorial governor. In 1862 the restless general was in a hurry to clean up the Indian problems so he could hurry back to Washington and earn medals and promotions in the Civil War.

"Six or eight years before that, your famous Mormon gunfighter, Porter Rockwell, had guided a survey party through Delta and Ely to lay out a new route that later became Highway 50. The reason for doing it was all the Indian problems settlers were having along the Humboldt River

31

Valley in the Elko area. The Indians up there were just too damn mean. And no amount of treaties, gifts and police actions could put the lid on them.

"Originally, Johnston's intent was to pacify, or kick the daylights out of, the Indians along the Humboldt because they were the ones causing most of the problems.

"But, as I said, Johnston was in a hurry to get back to Washington. So when he was camped at Fish Springs, about 40 miles northeast of here, and found out there was a large Indian camp down in Pleasant Valley, the general saw a chance for a quick and easy victory that would allow him to get back to Washington ahead of schedule—with a few hundred scalps hanging on his belt. He knew the Indians in Pleasant Valley were mostly Goshutes, not respected for fierce fighting skills. The Goshutes had never possessed very many horses. But things like that were easy to cover up in a report to Washington. Johnston was sure a fight with the Goshutes would be an easy one, and over with quickly, and no one in Washington would ever know the difference.

"Now you have to be careful reading Nick Wilson's account. He was on Johnston's payroll, and sympathetic with the Army side of things. Wilson said there were 300 warriors gathered below us here getting ready to wipe out all the stage stations along the immigrant route.

"But eyewitness accounts of the battle, including Wilson's, suggest beyond a reasonable doubt that the people here did not comprise a warrior camp. Instead, there were a lot of families with women, children and old people just wanting to mind their own business. I don't doubt there were warriors here, too, who were harassing immigrants, and who intended to continue doing so.

"The reports say some of the soldiers were killed by women, that five- and six-year-old children fought like wildcats, that papooses were scampering into the bulrushes along the lake to hide, that dogs were barking. Warriors going to battle did not take women, children, babies, old people and dogs with them. This was not a warrior camp."

Chapter 3

Emmett pointed toward the Kern Mountains across the valley. "See the draw to the left of the highest peaks?" he asked.

"Yes."

"There is a good spring just beyond. We call it Upper Sulphur Spring. The canyon leading to the spring is very rugged. It is called Skinner Canyon, and it fits Wilson's description of the rugged canyon he led the soldiers up the day before the battle. They camped at a spring at the top of the canyon, probably Upper Sulphur Spring. Wilson describes Johnston and his lieutenants climbing the nearby peaks to watch the Indian camp the day before the battle. He was probably referring to those peaks on the right side of the draw. There is a very steep Indian trail in the draw. Wilson describes three pack mules rolling to their deaths as the Army came down the mountain during the night just prior to the morning attack. We could ride up there on the horses some time, if you want to. I don't think Roberts has been up there."

"Were there any survivors?" Ella asked.

"About three hundred soldiers, but according to the Army report, there were no Indian survivors. Not one."

"How can that be? Surely, after the battle was over, someone would find a woman in the brush with a bullet in her shoulder, or an infant under a blanket."

"The order of the day was that there would be no survivors. So those like you described were shot, stabbed, or clubbed to death."

"Killing helpless people is murder," she said.

"You and I call it that, but not the Army, at least not in 1862."

"Did General Johnston get a medal?"

"I don't know, but he did get an assignment with the Union Army that got him killed."

"Before we get on our horses and ride back," Ella said slowly, "I have one more question."

"What is it?"

33

"When we were down by the house, you eloquently described this valley as a healing place. Up here you have just as eloquently described it as a killing place, even a murdering place. How can it be a murdering place and a healing place at the same time? I am sitting here looking over a beautiful valley. What kind of place is it?"

"The battle took place before smokeless gunpowder was invented," Emmett explained. "During the early stages of the fight, Wilson said the smoke from the discharging firearms was so thick he couldn't see what was going on. Surely some of the Indians were able to get away. Look over the valley. See the rocky draws, the patches of brush, the juniper-covered sidehills. Some of the Indians must have found hiding places. And probably some of the wounded pretended to be dead so they would not receive further injuries.

"After the soldiers left, those who had been hiding came out to mourn the dead. Of those who survived, many were undoubtedly wounded. Some survived. Some did not. But one thing is sure, the suffering that transpired here is immeasurable. Perhaps that suffering, combined with the blood of those who died, sanctified this place as the healing place it is today. Perhaps it was a healing place before the battle. Perhaps the spirits of some of those who died here linger, not wanting others to suffer as they did, thereby adding to the spirit of healing that exists here. I do not know, only that it is so. Would you like to go back now?"

Ella nodded. They got to their feet and walked to the horses. They rode in silence back to the ranch.

Chapter 4

Little was said as Emmett and Ella unsaddled the horses. She knew it was time for her to leave, but found herself wishing she could stay longer. She liked Emmett Hays. He was hardened to the rugged outdoor life, but still sensitive to the horrible massacre that had taken place on his land so long ago. But he seemed too protective of his personal life, almost like he was trying to hide something. Ella had found what seemed to her a fascinating mystery, one she would probably never solve.

"Where will you go now?" Emmett asked, when the horses were put away.

"I think I'll continue around the mountains to Ibapah," she responded. "Is there a gas station and motel there?"

"There are two beer stations where you can buy gas, but no motels."

"Beer stations?" she questioned. "I've never heard that term before."

"The signs in front of the two stores say 'beer and gas,' in that order. The population of Ibapah is about two hundred people, but the two stores sell 300 to 500 cases of beer a month—all Budweiser. I think Ibapah is the only place in America where alcohol consumption exceeds gasoline consumption."

"You're not serious," Ella said. "I thought it was illegal to sell beer on Indian reservations."

"I think it is, but Ibapah is not on the Goshute reservation, just at the edge of it."

"Aren't the tribal leaders concerned?" she asked.

"I'm sure they are," he responded.

"Why don't they do something about it?"

"Like what? If people want to drink, they drink."

"But why so much?"

"I don't know. The government gives them housing, commodities and a monthly allowance. The more the government gives them, the more they seem to drink. But as soon as somebody suggests cutting back the monthly allowance so they can't buy so much beer, the whole tribe is on the warpath, including the leaders who know better than anyone else how bad the situation is."

"What's the answer?"

"I don't know. Maybe after you finish your piece on the massacre, you ought to write about alcohol abuse on the Goshute reservation, or reservations in general. It seems to be a universal problem. Maybe you could write a whole book. I've thought of doing it myself."

"Maybe I'll do that," Ella said. "I'm looking forward to going there."

"Only problem is you won't be able to go the way you planned," Emmett explained. "There's a big pond in the road up by Blue Mass. Rain filled it a couple of days ago. The grader hasn't moved the dirt to drain it yet. You'll have to go back down in the valley, up to Callao and over Gold Hill."

"Is it farther that way?"

"Quite a bit."

"I have less than a quarter of a tank of gas."

"You'll never make it."

36

Chapter 4

"Can I make it back to Delta?"

"No, but you might get to the Border Inn on Highway 50. But with night coming on, it's not worth the gamble. Let me give you some gas out of my tank."

"Thank you. I insist on paying for it."

"Then I won't give you any." Emmett was looking directly into Ella's eyes now and smiling in a teasing kind of way. But she knew he meant what he said. He would not let her pay for gas.

Ella got in the Jeep and backed up to the overhead gas tank located next to the granary. She turned off the motor and got out as Emmett turned on the valve at the bottom of the tank, removed the nozzle from its resting place, removed her Jeep's gas cap, and inserted the nozzle. She could hear what sounded like a trickle, then all was quiet.

"We have a problem," Emmett said. "Seems the tank just ran out of gas. Knew it was getting low. Already ordered more. The tank truck will be here in the morning. But I guess that won't do you any good tonight."

"What about the neighbor down the road?" Ella asked, remembering the other ranch house she had seen before reaching Emmett's place.

"They went to Provo this morning. Won't get home until tomorrow night. They keep a lock on their fuel tanks."

"Is there anybody else?"

"Nobody close enough where you wouldn't be taking a chance running out."

"What do you think I should do?" she asked.

"Without giving it a lot of thought," he said, rubbing his chin thoughtfully, "I see two alternatives. One, you can stay here. You can have the entire upstairs to yourself. Or even better, you can stay in the bunkhouse. There's a lock on the door. You'll be safe."

Ella noticed her palms were sweating, and there were goosebumps on her forearms. She believed Emmett when he said she would be safe.

"What's the other alternative?" she asked.

"As soon as I'm through feeding I could follow you to the Border Inn. If you ran out of gas, I'd be right behind you to pick you up."

"That'd be a hundred-mile round trip for you," she said. "You would be willing to do that?"

"Yes," Emmett said simply, "but with two reservations."

"And what might they be?" she asked.

"I've got 30 first-calf heifers just starting to calve," he said. "Don't like to leave them for more than a few hours at a time, especially in the evening."

"Why?"

"Cows are like humans in that the first pregnancy is usually the most difficult. If help isn't handy, sometimes the calf will die, or the cow, too. You may not have noticed, but I checked them as we entered the driveway. I checked them again before we went riding, and again when we returned."

"You said there were two reasons for your reluctance to follow me to the Border Inn," Ella continued.

"The other reason is in the corral by the granary," he said. "Got a cow in there, number 53. She's had a prolapse and is about to calve."

"What's a prolapse?"

"Come here, I'll show you," he said as they began walking towards the corral.

"Cows are like women," he continued. "Some women in the later stages of pregnancy are inclined towards hemorrhoids. Cows have prolapses. Instead of the digestive tract trying to push out of the body, in cows it's the vagina. Somehow the lining comes loose and it pushes out through the opening. Looks like a cantaloupe or small balloon."

"Sounds awful," Ella said. "But I don't see anything like that on 53." They were standing by the fence looking at the cow, a hereford with a white face.

"I've already treated her," he explained. "Pushed everything back inside, then sewed the lips together so the vaginal wall can't come out again." Ella could see the orange twine, holding the cow together in two or three big stitches.

"Her milk bag is full," Emmett continued. "That tells me she is about to calve, about to go into labor."

"But how can she when she's all sewed up?" Ella asked.

"When she goes into labor I'll cut the stitches, and the calf will slip right out. If I'm not around to cut the stitches, the calf can't come out and the cow and calf will die, a good reason for not wanting to be gone for any length of time, especially in the evening."

"Why are cows more likely to calve in the evening?" she asked.

"Management. I feed them at night, just before I go to bed. While they are eating, and afterwards, while they are contentedly chewing their cud, is the time when they are least likely to go into labor. When daylight comes, they get up and start moving about. Not many go into labor in the mornings. That's a good time for me to leave, if I have to. But as the day progresses, they start to get hungry, and grow more restless. This is when most will go into labor. Because of the feeding schedule, most will calve in the late afternoon and evening. I don't like them to calve in the middle of the night."

"If 53 could talk," Ella speculated. "I suppose she would vote for you to stay here instead of following me to the Border Inn."

"I'm sure she would," Emmett responded.

"Then for her sake, maybe you should not leave," she said.

"Does that mean you will spend the night?" he asked.

"Yes," she said calmly, trying to hide her delight. "Maybe in the morning, before the tank truck arrives, you could show me where you think General Johnston and his men camped before the battle."

"I would like that," he said.

When he showed her the bunkhouse, Ella decided that's where she wanted to stay. Emmett told her that many years ago it had been a church and school down in the valley. It had hardwood floors, a kitchenette with a sink, a microwave and refrigerator, an oak table and chairs, a wood-burning stove, a sofa with a colorful Indian rug in front of it, three bunk beds, a private bedroom, and a bath with a shower. Everything looked new, except the old blackboard and chalk tray extending the full length of one wall. The other three walls contained continuous panes of white-trimmed windows.

Emmett helped Ella bring her things into the bunkhouse—a sleeping bag, coat, and a gym bag containing personal belongings.

"What's for supper?" she asked. "I have a good assortment of junk food in the car."

"How about wild rice stir fry and broiled mountain trout?" he asked.

"I thought cattle ranchers ate T-bone steaks and fried potatoes," she said.

"Usually do," he responded. "But when I was in town the other day I bought some fresh mushrooms, green peppers, cabbage, and broccoli. Haven't had a chance to cook any of it yet. Having you here is a good excuse to cook it all."

"What would you have had tonight if I wasn't here?" she asked.

"A Banquet TV dinner," he answered without enthusiasm.

"A TV dinner would satisfy me," she said, trying to be helpful.

"Having company is a good reason to cook a real meal," he explained. "Please indulge me."

"Then wild rice stir fry it is," she said. "Is there anything I can do to help?"

"Would you like to get the fish while I start preparing the rice and vegetables?" he asked.

"Sure, where's the freezer?"

"They're not in the freezer."

"In the refrigerator?"

"They're not there either."

Chapter 4

She sensed he was playing some kind of game with her. "Where are the fish?" she asked.

"In the pond. You have to catch them," he laughed.

"I thought you wanted to eat today," she said. "I'm not much of a fisherman."

"It's easy," he said. "I'll show you." He grabbed a fishing pole from behind the door, and a coffee can from under the sink. It contained plus-shaped kibbles. Ella followed Emmett up a little hill, just west of the bunkhouse.

"It's not very big," he said, as they stood at the edge of the pond, "but it's twelve feet deep. The fish grow big." He handed her the can with instructions for her to throw a handful of kibbles into the middle of the pond while he baited the hook.

"Looks like cat food. Are we going to be catching catfish?" she asked, looking into the can.

"It is cat food," he said. "The trout love it."

"Why don't you feed them fish food?" she asked as she threw a handful into the pond. The surface of the water began to boil as a dozen fish broke the surface of the water simultaneously in a frantic effort to gobble up the floating kibbles.

"Two reasons for using cat food," he explained. "First, it floats. Most fish food sinks to the bottom, some of it getting lost in the moss and silt. The second reason is the shape. Plus-shaped kibbles are easy to tie onto hooks."

For the first time Ella noticed Emmett had tied one of the kibbles onto the hook.

"It doesn't seem fair," she said, "getting them all excited to eat cat food, then slipping one in with a hook on it."

"It's called chumming," he said. "It's illegal on public waters, but dinner will be served on time at the Medicine Springs Ranch, even with an inexperienced hand reeling in the main course."

He cast the hook into the middle of the pond and handed the pole to Ella. As soon as she took it, the hook and piece of floating cat food disappeared beneath the surface of the water.

"You've got one, start reeling," he whispered. Frantically, she began to turn the handle on the reel.

"Easy," he cautioned, still whispering. "Just keep the line tight. You don't need to hurry. Tip up, line tight. That's all. Easy. Easy."

A minute later a 14-inch trout was flopping about on the grassy bank. Ella found herself wishing the pond was four times as large so the reeling part would last longer. She liked the feel of Emmett standing close, whispering to her as she pulled in the supper they were going to share.

Ella watched Emmett's strong, brown hands, rough from the rigors of ranch work but quick and sure as they removed the hook from the fish's mouth and tied on another piece of cat food. She resisted the urge to reach out and touch those hands—then felt embarrassed that she, a married woman, would even think such a thing.

The second time, Emmett encouraged Ella to cast the line into the water. She felt awkward and unsure of herself, but tried anyway. The hook didn't go halfway to the middle, but it didn't matter. A fish grabbed it anyway.

"Tip up, line tight, easy, easy," were again the soothing words that guided the fish to shore.

Ella returned to the bunkhouse to wash up while Emmett cleaned the fish and went to the main house to start the rice and vegetables.

As an afterthought Ella decided to take a quick shower. As she did so she couldn't help but wonder how many times Emmett had showered in the bunkhouse, standing exactly where she was standing now.

Realizing she was allowing her thoughts to wander into forbidden territory, Ella turned the faucet to cold. Still, when she stepped out of the shower stall, she couldn't be sure the out-of-breath feeling was totally the result of cold water. When she dressed, she put the same jeans and sneakers back on, but replaced the green blouse she had been wearing with a light blue sweatshirt, a plain one with nothing printed on it. When she entered the house, the out-of-breath feeling returned. Emmett was in his stocking feet, coming from the kitchen to greet her. He was wearing a white T-shirt. Ella couldn't help but notice the well-defined muscles in his arms. He moved with the grace of a cat.

For the first time since Ella had met Emmett Hays, he was not wearing a hat. He looked different—still handsome, but different. His steel-gray eyes held the same intensity, but without his hat he looked undressed, more casual. Perhaps the effect was created by the contrast in skin color. While his cheeks, chin, and neck had a healthy tan, his forehead, used to the protection of the black hat, was white. He had more hair than she would have guessed, sandy in color with streaks of silver.

He held a knife in his hand, a stainless steel blade with a black handle, but she felt no fear.

"The vegetables are washed, cut and ready," Emmett explained cheerfully. "Think I'll take a quick shower while the rice steams. Make yourself at home. Look around, if you like. Maybe you can put on a CD."

"I'll do that," she said, as he disappeared into the back of the house.

As Ella stepped from the entryway into the kitchen she could smell the cooking rice. On the butcher block table in the center of the kitchen were neat little piles of chopped mushrooms, green peppers, green onions, broccoli, and cabbage. On the counter next to the table was a jar of olive oil, some white cooking wine, ginger, soy sauce, salt, pepper, brown sugar, a bag of sliced almonds, and a shaker of Shillings broiled steak seasoning. Obviously Emmett Hays was as comfortable in the kitchen as he was on the range with cattle and horses.

Ella stepped into the living room. The decor was typical ranch, wood and stone walls, rustic furniture, Navajo rugs—nothing fancy or rich, just good taste. On the east wall was a large C.M. Russell painting of two cowboys roping a grizzly bear.

On the west wall were two nickel one-armed bandits, reminding her she was in Nevada. A closer look revealed these were no ordinary slot machines. The closest one, instead of having the usual drawings of bars, cherries and plums on the cylinders, had pictures of local outlaws and gunfighters—Butch Cassidy, The Sundance Kid, Porter Rockwell, and an Indian horse thief named Walkara.

She decided Emmett Hays had a creative side, but he carried it too far on the second slot machine. The cylinders were covered with pictures of early Mormon historical figures—Joseph Smith, Brigham Young, and John Taylor. She decided to tell Emmett she didn't appreciate his taste in slot machine art.

She stepped from the living room into a large family room area, apparently a newer addition to the rest of the house. On the far side were windows looking out on the Deep Creek Mountains. On the near side, where the ceiling was higher, were game trophies, including a buck mule deer, bull elk, antelope, two pheasants, and a hawk.

At one end of the room was a large dining table, opposite a doorway leading back into the kitchen. At the other end was an entertainment center surrounded by sofas and easy chairs. In the far corner was a television and VCR with an abundant assortment of western videos, and the CD player Emmett had mentioned.

Ella started looking through the CDs, and was startled by what she found—one containing George Strait songs. Emmett had deceived her when he indicated he was not familiar with George Strait. Or was this Emmett's way of teasing her? Maybe it didn't really matter. But if he could deceive her once, maybe he would do it again. She would have to be careful.

When Emmett emerged from the bathroom at the end of the hall beyond the big table, the room was full of the sound of George Strait singing one of his latest hits. Emmett was wearing clean jeans, white socks, and a long-sleeved tan shirt

Chapter 4

as he walked towards her across the carpet.

"Who is singing?" Ella asked, trying to catch him off guard.

"Gene Autry?" he asked, taking no time to think. "Or is it one of the new Confederate Railroad songs?" He didn't wait for her to answer, but hurried into the kitchen to check the rice. Following him, she decided to drop the subject.

"Such a pleasant evening, the first warm one, thought we could cook and eat outside," Emmett suggested. "Do you mind?"

"No, not at all. That would be nice. By the way, I think your slot machine, the one with the church leaders on it, is pretty tacky."

"Actually, it's very educational," he responded, undaunted by her criticism as he carefully pushed the piles of vegetables onto a platter so he could take them outside.

"But the slot machine is a gambling device, something the Church is opposed to," Ella protested.

"This one is no gambling device," he argued. "When you are through playing with it you can reach around back and get your nickels back. As well as being educational, it's a great babysitter."

"You have to admit, it's still offensive, even repulsive, to a lot of people," she added.

"That's half the fun of having it," he shot back as he tossed her a red tablecloth, then hurried out the door, his strong arms loaded with food and cooking gear. She shrugged her shoulders and followed.

Ella spread the tablecloth on the pine picnic table located under the big trees on the east side of the house. She arranged the eating utensils while Emmett lit a fire under a steel grill resting on some large rocks. He placed a skillet on the grill and poured some olive oil into it. By the time the pan was hot, the flames had diminished sufficiently to allow him to place the two trout directly on the grill. He sprinkled some of the Shillings steak seasoning on the fish. Rather than ask him why he seasoned fish with steak seasoning, Ella decided

45

to wait and see how the fish tasted.

Next, Emmett dumped the mushrooms, green peppers, onions, broccoli and cabbage into the hot oil. Using a wooden spoon, he mixed everything together in the sizzling oil. He dumped the already-cooked wild rice into the pan, then added the seasonings, first the wine, then the soy sauce. He sprinkled on the ginger and brown sugar. Last, he added the sliced almonds.

After he had thoroughly stirred the contents of the pan one more time, Emmett sprinkled on a generous portion of grated mozzarella cheese.

He turned the fish, sprinkled on more steak seasoning, then removed the heavy skillet from the grill and placed it in the middle of the table. A minute later he placed a fish on each plate. Dinner was ready. Ella and Emmett seated themselves on opposite sides of the table.

"It's nice to have someone to share my dinner with," he said, nodding for her to begin eating. Ella stabbed a big piece of mushroom and placed it in her mouth, chewing slowly, looking beyond Emmett at the evening shadows on the mountains, savoring the taste of the mushroom, and the mood of an April evening out-of-doors.

"How long have you been alone?" she asked, hoping he would talk about himself. She speared another mushroom and placed it on her tongue.

"Sometimes I think it has been too long," Emmett said slowly, "like when I look across the table at you. But when I look up at the mountains I feel like it has not been long enough."

"I don't understand."

"Healing takes time. I don't understand either. Let's change the subject," he said, his voice suddenly becoming more confident and cheerful. "I assume you like mushrooms."

"I love mushrooms," Ella said, "and these are some of the best I have tasted. You are an excellent cook."

"You like them best, so you eat them first," he

46

observed.

"Is there anything wrong with that?"

"When you were a child, and your mother served you a piece of cake with yummy marshmallow frosting, did you eat the frosting first?"

"Of course."

"When you eat a T-bone steak, I assume you eat the smaller, tender filet side before the tougher New York side."

"Looks like you've got me all figured out," Ella said, the tone in her voice more cool.

"After a hard day at school," Emmett continued, "let's say you stop by the grocery store on the way home. You see a video you have wanted to watch, but you are hesitant to check it out because you have a pile of papers that need grading. But you check out the video anyway, telling yourself it will help you relax and wind down."

"I've done that," she admitted. "More than once."

"I'll tell you what you do after dinner," he said confidently, using his fingers to put a piece of pink fish in his mouth. "You watch the video before you correct the papers."

"As I said before, you've got me all figured out," Ella responded. "If you're so smart, tell me why this conversation is making me feel so rotten, like I'm standing before you in a swimming suit while you look at my varicose veins."

"You have varicose veins?" Emmett asked.

"No, but I probably will someday. That's something women my age worry about."

"Would you like my honest assessment of what you have been telling me about yourself?" he asked.

"I don't know if I could place any value in your assessment," she said. "Seems we have a situation where a cowboy is trying to tell a college professor how to run her life. Or are you really a psychiatrist disguised as a cowboy?"

"Then let's forget the whole thing," he said. "What do you want to talk about?"

"Let's talk about Emmett Hays," Ella said boldly. "Who is this man who is sharing his dinner with me?"

"You really want to know?"

"Yes."

"Then look at my plate. What do you see?"

"Food. You've eaten about half of it."

"Be specific. What kind of food do you see?"

"A fish with about half the meat still on the bones, some broccoli, cabbage, almonds, peppers, onions, and mushrooms—lots of pieces of mushrooms."

"Do you think I like mushrooms?"

"I don't know. You haven't indicated if you do, or if you don't. Maybe you don't like them, because so many are still on your plate."

"Do you think I would buy a whole bunch of mushrooms to put in a stir fry for myself if I didn't like them? Remember, I didn't know I was going to have company for dinner."

"I suppose not. I guess I can conclude then that Emmett Hays likes mushrooms. Whoopee! We have something in common."

"I like mushrooms, just as you do," he said, getting up from the table. "But I don't eat them first. When I cook a T-bone steak, I eat the tender filet part last. When my mother served me a piece of cake on my twelfth birthday, I remember saving the frosting until last. A month ago, I ordered through the mail the Clint Eastwood video, *Unforgiven*. The same day the video arrived I received a BLM range report that needed to be filled out and returned—about as much fun as grading papers. After supper I filled out the report, then I watched the video."

"What are you trying to tell me?" Ella asked, as she forked the last of her food, some cabbage and broccoli, into her mouth. "I hope you are not going to tell me that saving the best part until last is a key ingredient of successful and happy living."

"Sometimes in the past," he continued, ignoring her question, "when I've needed a hired hand, I've put an ad in the *Deseret News* or *Salt Lake Tribune*. The city boys come out, dressed in their Wrangler jeans and cowboy boots. They know how to ride, or they think they do. Some can even rope. In the course of the interview they want to know how many days off they get, how long the lunch hour is, all about the insurance benefits, how many hours a day they can practice roping, or if they can use your facilities to train their own horses. That's when I send them down the road and hire a Mexican or Peruvian, who doesn't like to go to town and will work all month for $700.

"I guess I'm talking about delaying gratification, scheduling pain before pleasure, work before play, toil before rest. It's the way I grew up, and bitter experience has taught me it is the only decent way to live. I see society going in the opposite direction—enjoy now, pay later, play before work, pleasure before pain."

Emmett was pacing back and forth, his right fist clenched, obviously very emotional about what he was saying. Ella remained quiet as he continued. "Delaying gratification is the process of scheduling the pain and pleasure in life in such a way as to make the pleasure better by facing the pain first and getting it over with."

"You're entitled to your opinion," she said. "I earned a Ph.D. watching videos before grading papers and doing homework. I earn $50,000 a year teaching at the university level. You can't exactly call me a failure because I like to eat my mushrooms first."

"I'm not calling you a failure," Emmett said. "As your cowboy therapist, I'm merely trying to open your eyes to a fault that if corrected would make you happier and more productive."

"Then please continue," Ella said, fighting the urge to argue.

"Sometimes in the morning I will make a list of the things I want to accomplish that day—replace an irrigation headgate, shoe a horse, discuss a water turn problem with a neighbor, or pack salt to a roadless area where I have cattle. I find that if I tackle the more difficult tasks first and get them

over with, I get a lot more done. Seems I spend an hour or
two fighting the hard tasks, then have the rest of the day to do
the things I like to do. On the other hand, if I do the pleasant
things first, saving the hardest for last, it seems the happy
things are finished in an hour or two, and I spend the rest of
the day fighting the hard tasks. I've done it both ways, and
trust me, doing the tough things first is the only decent way
to manage your day, and your life.''

"Thank you," Ella said quietly. "Maybe I will try it
your way, at least for a while. I don't think it will be easy."

"No, it won't. One of the worst, most false lessons I
ever learned, and unlearned, was when the odometer broke in
my Chevrolet Suburban. It stuck at 41,000 miles. Every time
I drove that vehicle for the next year, I reminded myself I
needed to take it in and fix the odometer, but I never did.
Then one day it started working again, and never missed a
mile until I sold it at 118,000 miles.

"What happened with the Suburban was a fluke. Life
is not that way. Problems do not fix themselves. They do not
go away if we avoid them long enough. If we start each day,
doing the easy things first, sometimes we never get to the
difficult tasks or problems. Unfortunately, the difficult tasks
are usually the most important, and because of their
importance should be addressed first. Do you understand what
I'm saying?''

"I think so," she responded.

"You Mormons believe the purpose in life is to become
like God. You think you are the only people in the world who
believe that, but you are not. The subject is discussed in detail
in one of the best-selling books in the world, *The Road Less
Traveled*, by Scott Peck.

"Becoming like God involves a tremendous growth
process, perhaps an infinite one. And growth involves, by its
very nature, struggle, pain and effort. Yet many people seem
to think life is supposed to be easy. The college student thinks
that as soon as he graduates life will be great. The single
woman thinks that as soon as she marries Prince Charming,

Chapter 4

she will live happily ever after. The rancher thinks that as
soon as he pays off the chattel loan, he will enjoy ranching.
It's as if people think life is supposed to be easy, as it is for
pigs and cattle in feedlots. But life's not that way. Buddha
taught 'Life is suffering,' as the first of the 'Four Noble
Truths.' Ben Franklin said, '... things that hurt, instruct.' A
common saying in executive circles today is, 'What doesn't
kill you, makes you stronger.'

"Life is hard. It's supposed to be that way. This is one
of life's great truths. Life is an endless series of problems,
and solving them is difficult. Only by realizing this great truth
can we transcend it. Once we accept the fact that life is
difficult, once we accept the fact that that's the way things
are, then life is no longer difficult, because the fact that life
is difficult no longer matters."

"You're not only a psychologist, but a philosopher
too—a cowboy who doesn't know George Strait, but can quote
Buddha. I'm impressed," Ella said.

"I'm a theologian too," he said, continuing to pace
back and forth in front of the table.

"What theological treasure do you wish to share with
me?" she asked.

"Just one. Do you know what the Devil's real name
is?" Emmett asked.

"Satan?"

"No. It starts with an L."

"Lucifer."

"Wrong again. It's laziness with a big L. Because of
laziness you watch a video before correcting papers. Laziness
stopped me from fixing the steering—I mean odometer—on
my car. Growth requires effort. Laziness is the biggest
obstacle to growth. Laziness is the Devil, the real enemy, and
he will destroy us if we let him." Emmett stopped pacing,
relaxed his fist.

"It's almost dark," he said, his voice quieter. "The
heifers need to be checked. Would you like to come with
me?"

51

The Moriah Confession

"Sure," Ella said, sensing Emmett's monologue had ended too abruptly. With all his apparent wisdom, it seemed he was trying to hide something from her. He didn't sound like a philosopher giving a lecture, but like a man in a life-or-death struggle with important personal issues.

A minute later, in the waning twilight, they were standing outside the heifer corral, looking in. Some of the heifers were eating. Others were standing, or lying down, most chewing their cud.

"What are you looking for?" she asked.

"A swollen bag is one of the first signs that a cow is about to calve," he explained. "Sometimes mucus starts oozing. Sometimes you can see a bulge at the back end where the calf is starting to push out. A cow starting labor will usually want to be by herself, maybe go off to a far corner of the corral. While some of the bags are swollen, I don't see any indication that we'll have a new calf in the next few hours."

After checking number 53 they returned to the house. It was dark now.

"What does your husband do?" Emmett asked.

"He works in the athletic department at BYU, mostly in the football program," she said, wondering why she felt uncomfortable.

"Has he ever shown you a scouting report on a player?" Emmett asked.

"He brings them home all the time. I used to pretend to be interested, but not anymore. Why should I care if a young man can run the 40-yard dash in five seconds, or bench press five hundred pounds?"

"Then you probably wouldn't be interested in the scouting reports I have on my bulls."

"Emmett, I don't like being teased. They don't do scouting reports on bulls. Who cares how fast a bull can run the 40-yard dash?"

"Rodeo clowns care. But actually, 40-yard dash speed is not one of the items on my scouting reports. Would you like to see?''

''Sure,'' Ella said cautiously, wondering if this was some kind of prank. Emmett walked over to a file cabinet and removed some papers. She stepped beside him to look. When their elbows touched, she quickly pulled away.

''EPD is the important thing here,'' he explained. ''Expected progeny differences. It gives the birth weight of the bull. Bulls with low birth weights will help produce calves with low birth weights, which makes it easier for cows to calve. This is especially important with first calf heifers.

''The next important number is wean weight, and the length of time between birth and weaning, usually seven months. With this information you can figure growth rate. A bull that gained three pounds a day between birth and weaning is more likely to pass on a rapid growth rate to his offspring than a bull that gained two pounds a day.''

''Why is all this important?'' Ella asked, not wanting to sound bored.

''In the fall, a 700-pound calf brings a more money than a 400-pound calf. If ten of your cows die during calving, you've lost all your profit anyway. These numbers are very important, but they get more interesting as we look further down the page.''

''Am I reading this right?'' she asked. ''You know the semen count on your bulls.''

''Sure, you want them to be as fertile as possible. Can't have one out there shooting blanks.''

''How do you count semen on a big bull?'' she asked, then tried to answer her own question, laughing as she did so. ''I know. You go out in the corral with a red flag. You have a picture of a sexy cow drawn on one side. You wave it at the bull. He charges. You shout Ole' and hold out a specimen cup as he gallops by.''

By now Emmett was laughing too.

''Actually, the real way it's done isn't nearly as romantic as you describe it,'' he said.

''I can believe that,'' she responded.

"The history and research involved in semen testing are fascinating, a rare example where research on human guinea pigs advanced the field of animal husbandry."

"I don't dare ask what kinds of experiments with people would help extract semen samples from bulls," Ella said.

"Actually, it happened quite by accident, in prisons, where death row inmates were being executed by electrocution."

"You've got to be pulling my leg," she said.

"Hold out your hand," Emmett said. She did so, palm up. Gently he placed his hand over hers. Both were looking at the touching hands.

"Several milliamps of electricity are passing back and forth between our hands," he explained. "If certain switches in your head are turned the right way, a sexual response is evoked."

Ella pulled her hand away and felt a blush coming on. She felt confused. She didn't want Emmett to know the switches in her head were turned the right way.

"If two or three milliamps can cause a mild sexual response, can you imagine what 10,000 full amps will do?"

"The climax that kills," Ella said, not sure if her comment was funny or serious. "I find it hard to believe that men who die in the electric chair experience sexual pleasure. I mean, since they die, how can anyone ever know what they've experienced?"

"When their clothes are removed for the autopsy," Emmett explained, "it's been discovered the victims were ejaculating as they died."

"How ironic. The legal system that thought it was punishing criminals by sending them to the electric chair was, in fact, giving them the ultimate sexual pleasure."

"It appears so. At any rate, scientists began wondering if a middle range dose of electricity, not strong enough to kill, might invoke sexual responses in animals. It did. The result was an electrical device which allows veterinarians to collect semen from bulls. It looks like a big crayon, about the size of a cowboy boot. The vet shoves it inside the back end of the bull until it touches the prostate gland, then turns on the juice. The bull's eyes cross, his tongue hangs out, and he starts ejaculating all over the place.

"The vet catches a couple of drops on a glass slide and puts it under the microscope. A minute later he has the sperm count. That's how it's done."

"Fascinating," Ella responded, not sure whether she should feel embarrassed, offended, or thankful for the free education she was getting in animal husbandry.

"I think it's time for me to hit the sack," she said. "It's been a long day, and I'm very tired."

"I'll walk you to the bunkhouse," he said. "Think I'll check the heifers again." Emmett grabbed a flashlight and a jacket, then opened the door for her.

It was a clear night, and there appeared to be thousands of stars in the clean desert sky. The breeze that had been blowing earlier in the evening had stopped. The air was warm, still and quiet. For an instant Ella thought she might ask Emmett if she could go with him to check the cows, but decided against it. Suddenly she felt very tired. The sleeping bag was going to feel wonderful.

"Thanks for putting me up, and feeding me dinner," she said sincerely, as they reached the steps to the bunkhouse.

"Thanks for hitting the deer so we could spend a day together," he answered. "It meant a lot to me. I don't think you'll ever know how much."

She thought about asking him why, but decided against it. She had had enough conversation with Emmett Hays for one day.

"Good night," she said as she stepped inside and closed the door behind her.

"Breakfast will be served at seven, and there won't be any mushrooms in the scrambled eggs," Emmett called after her. Five minutes later, Ella was sound asleep.

Chapter 5

Although Ella went to sleep quickly, exhausted from a long and eventful day, her sleep became restless and broken in the middle of the night. Her mind was filled with vivid images. They included vast stretches of uninhabited desert where there were no gas stations, majestic snow-capped mountain peaks, deer running in front of her Jeep, Emmett Hays riding into her life on the horse Geronimo, Emmett calling her a lady from Spanish Fork before she told him that's where she was from, cleaning the deer, the hermit's cabin, the battlefield with faded images of women and children desperately fighting and fleeing as soldiers shot, stabbed and clubbed them to death.

She could see cows, especially number 53, waiting to have their calves. She wondered if she should consider writing about alcohol abuse on the Goshute reservation. Maybe it wasn't as bad as Emmett said. She could see trout rising to grab pieces of cat food, fish roasting on a grill, a wild rice stir fry, a warm spring evening with a gentle breeze and a view of the rugged Deep Creek Mountains, and Emmett's more than enthusiastic lecture about mushrooms, frosting and T-bone steaks. Why had he been so emotionally involved in a lecture on procrastination and laziness? Ella was beginning to get the feeling he was a man who had suffered much, who was still suffering, but she had no idea what the cause might be. She could not guess why a cowboy would name a horse Tithing.

At one point Ella began wondering if she had locked the bunkhouse door before going to sleep. During the night Emmett would be getting up to check the cows. She didn't want him checking in on her, too. Or did she? Unable to remember if the door was locked, she finally got up and checked. It was locked. She left it that way.

It seemed like three nights had passed before Emmett finally called her to breakfast. Ella was wearing a dark green cotton shirt, clean jeans and white high-topped sneakers as she hurried across the yard to breakfast. The morning air was crisp, but not cold. The calm desert sky was deep blue, promising another pleasant spring day.

When Ella entered the kitchen she noticed Emmett was wearing the same tan shirt and jeans he had put on after his shower the night before.

"No new calves, and none of the cows look particularly uncomfortable," he said cheerfully. "The way's clear for a morning ride. How'd you sleep?"

"Good," she lied.

The breakfast was simple, with bacon, French toast, and orange juice—the best she had ever tasted. Had she been served the same juice in a fine restaurant she would have believed it had been flown in from Florida the night before, after being squeezed from the best tree-ripened oranges.

"Why is the orange juice so good?" Ella asked, thinking maybe he knew something she didn't about buying juice.

"I buy the frozen concentrate with extra pulp," he explained. "That gives it the texture of fresh juice. When I

Chapter 5

mix it, I stir in a third of a cup of sugar. That gives it the tree-ripened sweetness.''

''Were you a cook before you became a cowboy?'' she asked good-naturedly.

''No. Cooking is just a hobby, one that requires time and company.''

''What are your other hobbies?'' she asked.

''Entertaining college professors,'' he responded. Then Emmett suddenly got serious. ''I'm sorry about last night, the lecture about the mushrooms and all. I got carried away. I had no business telling you how to live your life. I apologize.''

''Accepted. But I've been thinking about what you said. It makes sense, a lot of sense, I think. I'll try it your way for a while, saving the best for last, eating the broccoli before the mushrooms.''

''Good,'' he said, getting up from the table. ''I'll do the dishes after you leave. If you'd like to check the cows one more time, I'll catch and saddle the horses.''

''I'm not sure,'' Ella said, hesitating. ''I might miss something. I have no experience at this. You'd better do it.''

''Trust your instincts,'' he said.

''What does that mean?'' she asked, beginning to feel frustrated.

''You are female, like the cows. You have delivered two offspring of your own. You should be more in tune with these cows and what they are going through than I am, even though I have more experience.''

''Do you really believe that?'' she asked.

''Sure, look closely at each cow, then let your feelings be your guide. Make a mental note of anything that seems unusual, and tell me about it. Chances are you won't see anything out of the ordinary.'' He turned and headed out the door. Ella followed, then went in the opposite direction, to the corral holding the first-calf heifers, wondering how Emmett knew about her having two children. She couldn't remember telling him that.

Fifteen minutes later she walked up to Emmett as he

59

was tightening the cinch on Tithing.

"How do the heifers look?" he asked.

"Fine, but one looked like it might be calving. I need to ask you something that might seem stupid."

"Go ahead."

"Do baby calves have big yellow teeth?"

"No. Their teeth are white and perfect."

"How big are their teeth?" she asked.

"Small, proportionate to the size of the head."

"So they are not born with teeth as big as their mother's, and yellow?"

"No. What did you see?" Emmett asked, really curious now. He turned to look at Ella.

"One of the cows. She's holding her tail out. It looks like some big, yellow teeth are starting to come out of her back end."

"All the better to eat you with," he laughed.

"But you said the head came first," she said. "Wouldn't the head be preceded by teeth?"

"Actually, the head usually precedes the back end. But the head is normally preceded by the front feet, not teeth. The hooves are usually yellow, and I suppose they look like teeth. You saw a cow in the early stages of labor. Let's go see. If the calf comes quickly, we might still get in our horseback ride."

When they reached the corral, the cow was still standing. By now, both front hooves of the new calf and two or three inches of leg were sticking out. The cow was obviously very uncomfortable. Her tail was sticking straight out, her back humped in discomfort. She had stopped chewing her cud, and was walking along the corral fence, looking for a way out.

"What do we do now?" Ella asked.

"Just wait, see what happens. If the calf doesn't come on its own, we'll have to pull it. Because the front feet are sticking out, we know it's not breech. That's good."

"Shouldn't we give her some anesthesia?" Ella asked.

"Some what?"

"You know, painkiller."

"No. She's a cow. Nobody does it."

The cow went down, then got up again. Emmett suggested they move away from the fence, thinking their presence might be making the cow unnecessarily nervous.

While they were waiting, Ella asked Emmett about his brand which was on the left hip of all the cattle and horses.

"My brand is another strange coincidence, like me knowing you were from Spanish Fork before you told me," he said as he picked up a twig and began to draw the brand in the dirt. Emmett said he called it the Box Double E, and it was the same brand Butch Cassidy registered in Wyoming in the 1880s. He drew a square in the dirt, then three lines off the right side and three lines off the left side. He showed Ella how Butch used the brand in a laundering operation for cattle rustlers, and how the young outlaw used his running iron to make eighteen or nineteen other brands of the period look just like his, enabling him and his men to sell stolen cattle.

"So what is the strange coincidence?" Ella asked.

"It has two Es in it, one for Emmett and one for Ella, a backwards E and a frontwards E," he explained.

"Which of us is the backwards E?" she asked.

"Me, of course," he said, reaching out with the stick and making a little plus sign in the middle of the box, between the two Es.

A little while later the cow went down again. The calf's feet were sticking out about six inches now. Emmett was beginning to believe the delivery was taking too much time. He said that sometimes in lengthy deliveries the calf could suffocate while coming through the pelvic area. He walked over to the fence and picked up a stainless steel contraption that looked something like a bumper jack. He told Ella it was a calf puller, and showed her how it worked.

Finally, the cow went down on her side and did not get up. She was having labor spasms, but the feet would not come out any further.

It seemed to Ella that hours had passed when Emmett finally announced it was time to pull the calf.

"I want you to help," he said as he climbed over the fence. She handed him the calf puller, then followed.

When they were behind the cow, Emmett showed Ella how to hold the puller, one end against the upper part of the cow's hind legs. He told Ella to keep it steady while he dropped to his knees and secured a front foot to each of the two ropes attached to the puller. When he finished, he pulled a disposable plastic glove from his pocket and pulled it over his left hand and forearm, then slipped his hand inside the cow to make sure the head was in the proper place behind the front feet. It was.

"Start cranking," Emmett said, after he had removed his hand and discarded the glove.

When Ella pushed the handle forward, one of the ropes pulled tighter. When she pulled the handle back, the second rope pulled. As she cranked the handle back and forth, the feet were pulled towards her in a seesaw motion.

Ella cranked the handle until the tension in the puller seemed sufficient that the ropes might break, or worse, that one or both of the calf's feet might be pulled off. She stopped.

" Maybe a C-section is in order," she suggested.

"Crank some more," Emmett ordered. She obeyed, using all her strength to push the handle down again. It didn't seem the feet were moving at all.

"Again, crank it again," he barked. She did it, this time using both hands to pull the handle back. Suddenly the tension in the puller was gone, causing Ella to lose her balance and fall to her knees, as a wet, red calf slipped halfway out of the cow. Emmett grabbed the calf by the front feet and pulled it the rest of the way out. After checking the mouth and nose for afterbirth and fluid, he straddled the calf, grabbed it around the middle, and pulled it up between his legs, vigorously shaking the excess liquid from its nose and mouth. Next, he rubbed the neck and back with his strong hands, then lowered the calf back to the ground. The wet calf was not bawling like a human baby, but it was breathing.

The cow was getting up now. Emmett grabbed the puller with one hand, and Ella with the other, and moved towards the fence as the mother turned to see her first baby. Looking and sniffing, she inched closer, until her head was directly over the baby. A minute later the cow extended her big, rough tongue and started licking the calf.

"Everything's fine," Emmett smiled. "You did a good job."

"It's beautiful," Ella said, still looking at the calf—so fresh and new, its big black eyes looking at the world for the first time.

"Yes it is, and I'll have three hundred of them before summer arrives."

"How many will have to be pulled?" she asked.

"Usually only two or three in a year," Emmett said as they started walking back to the house to clean up.

When they looked at the clock, they decided it was too late for the horseback ride. It was time for Ella to go.

"What if the tanker truck doesn't come?" she asked, as Emmett helped her put her things in her car.

"Then I guess you'll just have to stay," he teased. "A bunch of friends are coming over next Saturday to team rope. You could help keep score."

"Seriously," she said, "if the truck ..."

"Think I can rustle up some emergency gas, if you'll back your Jeep down below the granary."

Ella did so, and to her surprise, discovered two more gas tanks. As Emmett filled her tank, she realized he had known about this gas all along. He could have filled her tank the day before. He had tricked her into spending the night. She became angry.

"Emmett Hays, you are a cheat and a liar," she said, looking directly at him. "You said you were out of gas."

"I did not," he argued. "I said the other tank was empty, and that a tanker truck was supposed to come today. Both were true statements."

"Then you deceived me. I should have guessed you were capable of something like that when you said you didn't know who George Strait was. You probably lied about the massacre, too. I never want to see you again." Ella got in the Jeep and started the engine.

"Wait," Emmett called after her. Fortunately, her window was down. "If I had filled your tank yesterday, you would not have stayed."

"That is an absolutely true statement," she shot back. Ella put her hand on the gearshift and jerked it from park to drive. She pushed her finger on the button to close the window.

"This was supposed to happen," he shouted. "How did I know you were from Spanish Fork? I have two more article ideas for you. Who else can I get to help keep score at the roping next weekend?"

"That's your problem," Ella said, as she stepped on the accelerator and roared out of the driveway onto the road leading to Ibapah.

Chapter 6

The following Monday, after her one o'clock class, Ella walked over to the alumni house where her friend, Harriet, worked as an administrative assistant.

Harriet was free to leave her desk, so they went to the lunchroom for a cup of hot chocolate and a donut. Harriet was a woman who always welcomed an excuse for another donut—probably the main reason she had never married. While Harriet worked on her donuts, Ella gave a condensed version of the weekend in the west desert.

"I wouldn't waste any time on a man who will keep you overnight and not tell you if he's married, separated, divorced, widowed, or a confirmed bachelor," Harriet warned, when Ella had finished her story. "Not even if he looks like Tommy Lee Jones and rides a horse named Geronimo."

"He called me the lady from Spanish Fork before I told him that's where I was from," Ella explained. "He said something about me having two children before I told him about my family. It's like he already knows me. I keep wondering if perhaps he was a member of the faculty or administration at one time, or perhaps a student, though he wasn't in one of my classes. I would have remembered that.''

"So you want me to run a name search on Emmett Hays in my computer files?'' Harriet asked.

"Yes.''

"You know I'm not supposed to access those lists for personal reasons,'' Harriet cautioned.

"Absolutely. I wouldn't ask you to break any rules. I just thought that if you were already in a file on official business and just happened to be going through the h's, you might notice whether or not an Emmett Hays was listed. That's all.''

"As long as I don't have to break any rules, I'd be glad to keep an eye open,'' Harriet offered, winking slyly as she took another bite of donut.

"He runs cattle in Utah and has a horse named Tithing, but says he is not a member of the Mormon Church,'' Ella said, wanting even more from Harriet. "Perhaps he is lying, or perhaps he was a member at one time. If you are ever skimming through church records, or records of former church members ...''

"Wait a minute,'' Harriet interrupted. "This is the BYU alumni house in Provo, not LDS Church archives in Salt Lake City. There's a difference, you know. Those records are completely off-limits to people like me.''

"I know, I know. I was just wondering if you had a counterpart up there, someone who does work similar to what you do here. If so, you might suggest to that person that if he or she is ever in the records of former members and happens to be going through the h's ... That's all. I wouldn't want to get anyone in trouble.''

"Break's over,'' Harriet said cheerfully, shoving the last of the second donut in her mouth and pushing away from the table. "As far as I am concerned, this conversation never took place."

"Right," Ella said, trying to suppress her enthusiasm, knowing that if there was anything in BYU or church computers on Emmett Hays, it would be appearing on Harriet's terminal in the next 24 hours.

"Call me sometime," Ella said as she dropped Harriet off at her office.

"Maybe tomorrow," Harriet said coyly. The door to her boss's office was open.

The next morning, right after her ten o'clock class, Ella returned to her office to find a message to call Harriet.

"You had better sit down" were Harriet's first words when she recognized Ella's voice on the other end of the line. "What do you want first, the bad news or the good news?"

"How bad is the bad news?" Ella asked, almost regretting she had asked Harriet to help.

"Really bad, at least for you."

"Just tell me."

"He was a football player, a defensive back for BYU, in the early eighties."

"I don't believe you, and I don't appreciate your sense of humor," Ella fumed. "Next you'll be telling me he used to share a locker with my husband in the Richards Building."

"I'm not kidding, Ella. He played as a walk-on one year, and had a scholarship the next. Made five tackles."

"What's the good news?"

"He graduated with a major in psychology and a minor in history."

"Anything else?"

"Nothing after graduation, and that was more than 10 years ago. I have no idea how he knew you were from Spanish Fork and had two children."

"So that's all?"

"Not quite. A friend in Salt Lake accidentally stumbled onto an old membership record. Emmett Hays used to be a member of the Mormon Church. He served a mission in Mexico. He was married in the Manti Temple to a Jennifer

Williams. He was excommunicated for apostasy ..."

"Wait a minute. What does that mean?"

"Maybe something very innocent, like naming a horse Tithing or selling a car to a polygamist."

"I think you are too kind."

"Maybe so, but I've got to go. Come over for a donut sometime."

"Thank you. Goodby." Ella was glad Harriet didn't want to stay on the phone and talk about Emmett Hays. Ella needed time alone to digest this new information. She honestly thought she would be better off forgetting she had ever met the man. She went down to the Smith Fieldhouse and spent the rest of the afternoon running around the indoor track, hoping exercise might help push thoughts of Emmett Hays out of her mind.

That evening at supper, the conversation centered around speculation on who would be the standouts at the upcoming spring scrimmage for the BYU football team. While 13-year-old Kevin seemed interested by asking a few questions and making several cautious comments, 17-year-old Laura, for the most part, remained silent. Ella made several attempts to shift the conversation to the massacre site she had visited over the weekend, but George wasn't about to waste his time discussing what he called "a bunch of dead Indians" on the eve of the Pigskin Preview. It was an event, like the Super Bowl, that came around only once a year.

After supper, George announced he had to return to campus. A reporter from *Sports Illustrated* was coming to the scrimmage on Saturday and nobody knew why. A special brainstorming and planning meeting had been called.

"Why don't you just call the reporter and ask him why he's coming?" Ella suggested. "I can't imagine him wanting to keep the purpose of his visit a secret."

"So the English professor has suddenly become an expert on the complexities of sports information dissemination," George snapped back, obviously irritated that his wife would presume to understand, or attempt to simplify,

Chapter 6

what he considered the vastly deep and complex world of sports public relations. Without another word, Ella got up and left the room.

When George was gone, she went to her bedroom, closed the door, picked up the phone and called Emmett.

"Have you canceled next Saturday's roping?" she asked, when he came on the line.

"Why would I do that?"

"Saturday is Pigskin Preview day. As a former BYU football player you wouldn't want to miss that. Maybe you forgot your roping was on the same day."

"You're a better researcher than I thought," Emmett laughed. "How in the world did you find that out?"

"I work for BYU. Mormons are a record-keeping people. You ought to know that. You used to be one, too. Went on a mission to Mexico."

"You know it all," he said, his voice serious now.

"No. I don't know the meaning of apostasy, at least not in your case. And I don't know what happened to Jennifer."

"Do you want to know about Jennifer?" Emmett asked, his voice suddenly quiet, his words barely audible.

"Yes," Ella said, wondering why it felt so good to be the aggressor while someone else was scrambling to cover their behind.

"She was killed in a car wreck, three years ago."

Ella didn't feel good anymore. Unknowingly and unwittingly, she had ripped open a deep and tender wound. She felt like an insensitive creep.

"I'm sorry, Emmett. I didn't mean ..."

"It's all right. You would have found out sooner or later. I guess I didn't want it to be sooner. I don't know why. Can you come to the roping Saturday, and help us with the scorekeeping?"

Ella realized that if Emmett had asked if she was coming to the roping at the beginning of the conversation, she would probably have said no. But after bringing up the question about Jennifer, she didn't want to hurt him again.

"Yes," she said, with hesitation. "I'd like to come. What were the two article ideas you wanted to tell me about?"

"Oh, yes. The two ideas I was trying to express when you roared out of my driveway. Had the gate been closed, I think you would have crashed through it."

"So what are the ideas?"

"We have a lot of wild horses around here. Too many. It's a problem, a wonderful example of government waste and mismanagement, while a clear, economical solution is staring the government right in the face."

"Sounds interesting. I love horses. We'll talk some more about it when I come out. What's the other idea?"

"Few people know about the Moriah wilderness. Remember, I told you about the oldest trees in the world growing up there, and all the wildlife? If you are halfway competent with a camera, some of the rugged cliffs and canyons, with evening and morning shadows, would make some unbelievable photographs."

"I'm not a travel photojournalist," Ella said. "But maybe I'll become one. We'll talk about that more, too. What time do you want me there on Saturday?"

"Roping starts at nine, but why don't you come Friday night? You know your way around the bunkhouse."

"I won't have to share it with your roper friends?" she asked.

"Some might spend the night, but I'll make them stay in the house with me, or sleep in their trailers. The bunkhouse is yours."

"I'm looking forward to coming out," Ella said.

"I'm looking forward to having you," Emmett answered.

Starting to feel a growing awkwardness in the conversation, Ella said goodby and hung up the phone. She couldn't sleep that night, eagerly anticipating another weekend at the Medicine Springs Ranch.

The next morning, she decided she would not go. After

Chapter 6

school, she went to the mall and bought three boxes of candy. Every time a thought of Emmett entered her mind, she popped another piece of candy in her mouth, telling herself that if she gained 30 pounds, Emmett would find her unattractive, and the relationship would end without anyone having to exercise any willpower. She continued to shop as she stuffed herself with candy. She bought a new tennis racquet, and a cookbook she knew she would never use. By the time she left the mall, two of the candy boxes were empty.

But Friday morning her resolve melted. By the time she left for school, the Jeep was loaded with the things she would need in the desert. She told the children she had to do some more research for her article. She didn't tell George anything, knowing he was too involved in the Pigskin Preview to care what his wife was doing.

Chapter 7

"Tell me why a BYU football player doesn't want to go to the spring scrimmage," Ella asked, as Emmett was helping move her things from the Jeep to the bunkhouse. It was ten-thirty Friday night, and she had just arrived.

"Because I'm not playing," Emmett said.

"But there will be 10,000 people who are not playing either, who will show up and waste their Saturday watching it. Then there's my husband, who will spend two nights next week watching the video of the scrimmage. He can't play either, but he has to watch. Why doesn't Emmett Hays, the ex-BYU football player, want to watch the spring scrimmage?"

"Like I already said, I'm not playing. I guess I'm a bad sport. If I can't play, I don't want to watch. I would rather spend my Saturday roping steers. Doing something is better than watching someone else do something."

"Is roping steers better than playing football?" Ella asked. Emmett sat on one of the bunk beds and thought a minute before answering.

"Before I answer your question, I would like to share my feelings on spectator sports. I sense in you a hostility towards football, basketball and such."

"There's no hostility," Ella said. "I just think most spectator sports are dumb, and a waste of time and money."

"Life is not fair," Emmett began, his elbows on his knees. "The prostitute marries a congressman and founds an orphanage in India. The lady who never misses church ends up pushing a shopping cart down skid row. The brilliant Stanford medical researcher dies of AIDS. A good Christian dies of cancer while the drug dealer buys new houses for all his children after he pays for their college educations. A jerk in Orem inherits a piece of ground. A new mall comes in and makes him rich. He buys front row seats in Cougar Stadium, a condo at Sundance, supports a couple of missionaries and spends the rest of his life thinking he is better than everybody else, but he's still a jerk. Your husband loves football more than some of the coaches, but will he ever get a chance to be a coach? Probably not.

"Our government and legal system try to make life as just as possible. And life is sometimes fair, but we cannot count on it with any degree of consistency.

"The closest we get to true fairness is on the playing field, the world of athletic competition and spectator sports. Everybody plays by the same rules, using the same equipment, the same number of players on each team. Each team or player has an equal opportunity to score. There are officials to make sure the rules are enforced. Points and penalties are meticulously recorded. Because the environment on the playing field is as fair as we can possibly make it, the team with the most talent, the most practice, the best preparation, and the most focus usually wins. We go away from a well-played, well-officiated sporting event believing, or at least hoping, life is that way, too. Believing life is more fair than it really is, we are more willing to put our nose to the grindstone and work our guts out, believing in the end we

will get our just reward. Because of sports, and the fairness
we observe there, there is less rebellion, less suicide, less
unrest. Spectator sports are good for society."

"But not Emmett Hays," Ella stated.

"Actually, there are some striking similarities between
football and team roping," he said. "Catching a steer is like
catching a running back. You grab a ball carrier with your
hand instead of a rope, slow him down, turn him, then your
teammate comes in and finishes the job. I have the same
frustration when I miss a loop on a steer as when I used to
miss a tackle on a ball carrier. I feel the same adrenaline
surge when the chute opens and lets the steer out as when the
ball is snapped. The big difference is that in team roping, the
horse provides the speed and strength. All I bring to the show
are brains, balance, hand-eye coordination, timing and a
competitive spirit.

"The thrill of competing in football is over for most
young men in their mid-twenties, but I'll still be team roping
when I'm seventy—because I'll be able to buy a six-year-old
quarter horse fast and strong enough to catch and turn any
steer alive. Women don't have the speed and strength to play
football, but they make good team ropers."

"Because the horse provides the speed and strength,"
Ella said.

"You learn quickly," he responded. "Maybe you
should take up team roping. I'll give you your first lesson
tomorrow."

"At least it won't be an expensive hobby, like skiing or
flying."

"Wrong. It gets in your blood. It becomes a passion,
and an expensive one," Emmett explained. "Before you know
it, you'll have three or four horses valued at $3,000 each.
You'll buy a three-quarter ton pickup worth $20,000, a four-
horse trailer for about $5,000, ten practice steers at $500
each, your own practice arena on ground worth about
$10,000, $5,000 in fencing materials, a roping chute, saddles
and tack, and this is just to get started. You'll have several

hundred dollars in entry fees every time you compete, plus travel and lodging, and it'll probably be a few years before you win anything.

"But you can win. Ropers are ranked according to experience and skill levels, and you compete only against those who are at your skill level.

"I went to a roping once where my partner and I were competing against 150 teams. Each man paid $75 to enter. A pretty blond woman, roping with her husband, won a new horse trailer, a new saddle, and about $3,000 cash. She was a heeler, and the best roper in the arena that day. You could do that. Roping is intensely competitive, requires a lot of skill and luck, provides the adrenaline rush that accompanies power and speed, and is a lot of fun. You'll see it all in the morning."

"I can hardly wait," Ella said. "But I guess it's not a spectator sport. Crowds of people don't gather to watch team roping."

"Not usually. I suppose it's like square dancing, in that doing it is a lot more fun than watching it."

"Then you are not into spectator sports at all?" she asked.

"I drove 200 miles to watch Steve Young win the Super Bowl. I try to catch a BYU football game every year, and I even go to the local basketball rivalry when West Desert School plays Dugway. I like to watch sporting events, but life is too short to get all wrapped up in being a spectator. Doing is better, unless you are old, handicapped, or don't have anything better to do. I'd rather rope. Some of my friends say it is better than sex because you can do it 30 times in an afternoon. Anyway, glad you could come. Hope you sleep well. The ropers will start rolling in about eight—from Spring Valley, Callao, Snake Valley, Gandy, Garrison, Delta and Baker. The guys from Baker are tough, will take all our money, if we're not careful. See you in the morning."

"Good night," she said as Emmett disappeared out the door.

Chapter 7

Ella couldn't go to sleep. She knew Emmett was glad she had come, but still, she sensed that if he had to choose between her and spending time with his steers the next day, the steers would win.

But she was married to George, and Emmett had no business being involved with her as much as he was. Maybe she should have stayed home. Maybe there wasn't as much difference between Emmett and George as she had once thought. But if she had stayed home, she would be watching football instead of team roping the next morning. At least here she would be able to keep score. Ella was certain she was going to meet some interesting people.

But that wasn't good enough. She sat up in bed, her anger growing more fierce every second. Emmett's little speech about roping and how much he loved it made her feel secondhand, second place—the same way George had made her feel for so many years. She wasn't about to play second fiddle to a bunch of roping steers as she had to football. It didn't matter that Emmett wasn't her husband.

Ella pulled on her blue sweatshirt and slipped into her jeans and sneakers. Without tying the laces or brushing her hair, she turned on the light, marched out the door and across the yard to the big house. She didn't know what time it was, and didn't care. She banged on the door.

A minute later, Emmett appeared, rubbing his eyes, asking what was the matter. He was wearing his Wrangler jeans, nothing else, his belt and zipper undone.

"Come in," he said sleepily.

"No. I don't want to come in. I just want to ask you a question."

"It's the middle of the night. Can it wait until morning?"

"No."

"Go ahead, but make it quick. I've got to get up again in an hour or so to check the heifers."

Ella paused for a moment, wanting to make sure she selected the right words.

"If you had a choice tomorrow between roping steers or having a romantic adventure with me, which would you choose?"

"I'm not sure I understand your question," he responded sleepily.

"Emmett, don't give me any of your double-talk. Just answer the question, and answer it honestly. No jokes."

"You really want an honest answer, don't you?"

"Straight from the heart."

"OK. If I thought what you described would really happen tomorrow, I would pick up the phone right now, call everybody and cancel the roping."

"Do you really mean that?"

"If I thought there was a 50 percent chance of that happening, I would pick up the phone and cancel the roping."

"You do mean it."

"If I thought there was a 10 percent chance of that happening I would pick up the phone ..."

"That's all I wanted to know," Ella said, turning to walk back to the bunkhouse. For the first time there was a contented smile on her face.

"Wait a minute," Emmett called after her. "There is a question or two I would like to ask. Come back here." She turned around and started back.

"If I had answered your question differently, what then? If I had said, 'If you were waiting in the truck, the engine running, wanting to run off to Wendover and get married, I would have stayed in the arena until the last steer was roped and timed,' what would your reaction have been?"

"I wouldn't have been here when you got up in the morning," Ella said, turning back again to the bunkhouse.

"One more question," Emmett said. She stopped.

"Would you like me to get on the phone, call everybody and cancel the roping?" His voice was dead serious.

"You had better plan on a long and happy day of roping," Ella responded. She resumed her journey to the

Chapter 7

bunkhouse, leaving Emmett in the doorway scratching his head, struggling to understand what had just happened, wondering if maybe he was just having a bad dream. Or was it a good dream?

Chapter 8

About eight o'clock the trucks and trailers began pulling into the yard. Ella watched what was happening through the many bunkhouse windows as she was getting ready.

Most of the trucks were Fords, though there were a few Chevrolets and Dodges. Some of the trailers were aluminum, some steel, some two-horse, some four-horse, and one home-made job.

As soon as the vehicles stopped, the cowboys piled out, unloaded their horses, and began the saddling ritual. Some of the ropers were wearing cowboy hats, and some wore ball caps. Some wore T-shirts and some western shirts, but all wore Wrangler jeans, made obvious by the little brown patches over the back pockets. Ella decided to ask Emmett about that.

All but one of the ropers wore cowboy boots. The exception was a young Indian wearing high-top sneakers. There were two Spanish-speaking cowboys, whom she later learned were Peruvians working for The Thousand Peaks

Ranch, a large cow and sheep outfit. There were two women. She didn't know if they were ropers, or had just come with their men. They were dressed the same as the men, Wrangler jeans, too.

The saddling routine consisted of checking the feet and shoes on the horses, brushing, and attaching rubber bells or hoof protectors, shin-splints and other protective devices to the front legs below the knees. The saddle blankets, without exception, were thick and heavy. The western saddles were deeper seated than calf roping or bulldogging saddles, all with double cinches and breast collars. Every saddle horn was wrapped with black innertube rubber. There were tie-downs on all the horses, a strap extending from a noseband to the cinch to prevent the horse from throwing its nose up in the air.

Ella noticed two of the men using long black applicators to push big white pills deep into their horses' mouths. She wondered if they were giving the horses steroids, or some other kind of performance drug, to make them stronger and faster. Ella's list of questions was getting too long. It was time to locate Emmett.

She found him by the tack shed. He had just finished saddling Geronimo and Tithing.

"You missed breakfast," Emmett said, when he saw her coming.

"Sorry, I slept in. I'm not hungry, but I've been wondering what some of these horses have been served for breakfast, in the form of big white pills. Are they being drugged?"

"Roping horses are athletes, and just like human athletes, they sustain injuries of various kinds," he explained. "I'd bet if you asked your husband how many BYU football players near the end of a season are playing with some kind of injury, he'd say practically all of them, certainly more than half. And of those who are playing with injuries, most I would venture to say are taking some kind of pain medication. Those big pills you saw are pain pills for horses, and before ropings and rodeos you see a lot of them being shoved down horses' throats. The medication is called butte, or phenylbutazone. It works like Advil. The veterinarians say it is harmless and sometimes will prescribe up to four pills a day for a horse."

"Next question," she said.

"Shoot."

"Why is everyone wearing Wrangler jeans? I thought this was a roping, not a fashion show. I didn't think cowboys were such conformists."

"Actually, if you want to get technical, they are wearing Wrangler Pro-Rodeo jeans. I've never seen a professional rodeo cowboy who didn't wear them. It seems the Wrangler company went after the rodeo cowboy and his friends in a very aggressive manner, but with a practical approach. Feel the inside of my leg."

Ella hesitated.

"Don't be silly," he said, grabbing her hand and pulling it towards his leg. "Pinch the inside seam." She did so. "Now feel the outside seam." She did that too.

"The outside seam is a lot thicker," she said.

"They do that on purpose," Emmett explained. "When you do a lot of riding, the thin inside seam causes less wear and tear on your skin. When you spend a lot of time in the saddle, Wranglers are more comfortable."

"You sound like a salesman," Ella kidded.

"Now look at my back pocket," he continued. "Deeper than pockets in other jeans. My wallet doesn't come out. When I used to wear Levis, I'd lose my wallet a couple of times a year. Got to where I would never ride with a wallet in my pocket. With Wranglers, I have never lost a wallet."

"I'm sold. I'll buy a pair this week," she teased.

"Good. Now let me introduce you to some of my friends and neighbors. And, by the way, out here a neighbor is anyone living within a 50-mile radius, sometimes farther."

They walked over to the nearest truck and trailer, where a big, blond man with a round face and a swollen paunch was playing with a rope. He was wearing a black ball cap, and a white cotton glove on his right hand. He had a rope in one hand and a can of Coors beer in the other.

"Ella, meet Wade Hanks," Emmett said. "Runs sheep and cattle in lower Spring Valley. Won his first two cows in a poker game. Pulls the nuts out of sheep with his teeth. Named his white mule Jesus because it was so good while he was breaking it. Has a big heart, but a crude mouth.

"Wade, this is Ella Tanner," Emmett continued. "She's over from the BYU, writing an article. Better be careful what you say. Might find it on the front page of the *Church News*." Hanks smiled brightly, and took another deep drink from his can of Coors.

"I wonder if he perceived your words as a caution, or a dare," Ella speculated as she and Emmett walked to the next trailer.

"Probably a dare, but as I said, Wade has a good heart. One Christmas he got to feeling sorry for the Spanish and Peruvian herders. Lots of them out here, far from home for the holiday season. Wade went into Wells and found a Basque prostitute, and gave her $500 to make house calls to a list of about 20 herders on Christmas Eve. Before she took off to do her business, he dressed her in a buffalo skin coat and cowboy boots, nothing else. He wrote *feliz navidad* on her tummy with a red felt marker. That was the merriest Christmas the herders around here ever remember.

"Ella, meet Billy Thunder, a full-blooded Goshute from Ibapah, the best heeler in these parts," Emmett said as they approached the next trailer.

The handsome Native American smiled politely at Ella, but did not say anything.

"Billy gets the big one this month, when he turns 18," Emmett said.

"The big one?" she asked.

"Yes, the big check," Emmett explained. "As I understand it—correct me if I'm wrong, Billy—every Indian gets a check from the government each month, about $300.

Chapter 8

Some say it's payment for the land we stole from them. Others say it's welfare. Anyway, the Feds don't give the money to the kids. It goes in an interest-bearing account until the child turns 18, then he or she gets it all at once. In the next few weeks Billy will get a check for about $50,000."

"They give that kind of money to 18 year olds?" Ella asked, surprised. "Nobody ever thought to put it in a fund to help with schooling, starting businesses or buying homes? Who would be stupid enough to just give $50,000 to an 18 year old, no strings attached?"

"Our government," Emmett said, "but Billy is different than most. He has a plan. He's not going to blow his big one on new cars and drugs. He's got a herd of cows picked out, 75 bred heifers. He's trying to convince the tribe not to rent out its best winter and summer grazing to the local ranchers, but to start its own Goshute cattle ranch, with Billy helping to run it and providing the seed money for the first 75 animals. Because they have some of the best range in the state, it could be a profitable operation. I hope he succeeds."

"Are the tribal elders listening to you?" Ella asked Billy.

"I think so," he said with a slight Native American accent. "Some don't want change. Some don't trust my ability because I am young. I don't know what will happen."

"I wish you luck," Ella said, as she and Emmett moved to the next trailer.

"Think we are going to have to finish the introductions later," Emmett said. "Time to bring in the steers. Hop on Tithing and give me a hand."

A few minutes later they were galloping beyond the arena, through a fenced-in area below the road, into what Emmett called the bull pasture. The 15 steers they were looking for were bedded at the far end in some tall reed grass. It took only a minute to round them up and start pushing them back to the arena.

"These don't look like the rest of your cows," Ella observed.

"They're not cows, they're steers," Emmett said, correcting her.

"That isn't what I meant. They look like a different breed. They look like skinny mongrels—black, brown, spotted—they're all different."

"They're Corrientes, out of old Mexico. I get new ones every year."

"Why don't you rope your regular cattle?"

"Corrientes are tougher, run harder, last longer, don't get as big, and are more honest."

"Honest?" she asked. "You can't measure honesty in a cow."

"These are steers, not cows. When one runs straight down the arena, the same way, a hundred times in a row, I call him honest. Domestic cattle sour faster. That means they start ducking, stopping, turning right or left, or just refusing to run. They decide they don't like being roped, and refuse to cooperate. Corrientes, on the other hand, just keep running. I don't know if it is because they are dumber than domestic cattle, or just tougher. I like to call them honest."

"Corrientes, coming from Mexico, are probably cheaper than regular cattle, too," she added.

"It's the opposite, if you figure cost per pound," Emmett explained. "A good Corriente can cost half again as much as a domestic steer the same size."

Hearing a truck approaching from the west, Ella looked over her shoulder. A white Ford pulling a four-horse trailer was barreling down the road, just ahead of a huge cloud of dust. Two cowboys in black hats with long sideburns and handlebar mustaches were in the cab. Ella waved and smiled. They tipped their hats.

"My hell, the buckaroos have arrived," Emmett laughed.

"Buckaroos?" Ella questioned. She hadn't heard that term since she was a little girl going to the western movies at the Saturday matinee.

"Real cowboys, probably from the Geyser Ranch,"

Chapter 8

Emmett explained.

"I don't understand. I thought everybody coming to rope was a real cowboy."

"No. There's a big difference between a regular team roper and a buckaroo."

"Would you explain?"

"Sure. A buckaroo works on the big ranches, usually over a thousand cows. He ropes his horse out of the ramada before daylight and rides with the cows all day. Basically he does the same thing the old-time range cowboys did a hundred years ago. He tries to look just like them, and be like them in every way. He wouldn't be caught dead in a ball cap, or putting rubber on his saddle horn.

"When we have lunch today," Emmett continued, "the buckaroos probably won't eat on the same paper plates and use paper cups like the rest of us. They'll insist on tin plates and tin cups, the same utensils real cowboys used a hundred years ago.

"You saw the handlebar mustaches," Emmett continued. "They have stampede strings on their hats, and silk bandannas around their necks. They tuck their jeans inside their boots and wear big Mexican spurs. Sometimes they tie little bells on their spurs so everybody can hear them walking. They earn $700 a month, live in sheep camps in the summer, and bathe once a month."

"If I didn't know better," she said, "I would think you were jealous. Are you worried the real cowboys are going to win the money today?"

"I may be a little jealous of the romantic way they live, but I sure am not worried about them winning the money. If you could see Billy Thunder's face when the buckaroos drive through the gate, you'd see dollar signs in that Indian's eyes because he's already counting the money he's going to take from the buckaroos."

"I don't understand," Ella said. "I would think real cowboys, who worked every day with cattle, would be the best ropers."

"For one thing," Emmett said, "they are too caught up in tradition, and they don't have the time and money it takes to be really good in the arena when the event is being timed. For example, if you watched them unload their horses, you'd notice the mule hide instead of rubber on the saddle horns. That's great if you are going to rope a 2,000-pound bull and want to feed rope so your horse doesn't get jerked over. But roping Corrientes is a different story. The boys with mule hide will have to dally their ropes three or four times around the saddle horn before they can turn a steer. The boys with rubber on the horns only have to dally once before making the turn, and will have faster times.

"The buckaroos have 90 feet of soft rope. And I don't care what they say, it's real tough to consistently catch hind feet with a soft rope. A good arena roper needs only 35 feet of rope, and every good heeler uses a hard or medium-hard rope. All those extra coils the buckaroo carries get in the way.

"But a good roper can win, even with the wrong equipment," Emmett continued. "The simple truth is, the buckaroo, for the most part, is not a very good arena roper. Look at the way he lives. During good roping weather he works from sun up to sun down, sometimes seven days a week. Sure, he ropes a few cattle that need doctoring and such, maybe ten head in a good week. But when he's irrigating, putting up hay, or fixing fence, he doesn't rope at all. All summer, he might rope 50 head.

"On the other hand, look at Jim over there, on the paint horse. He lives in Baker and drives a road grader for the county. He's what the buckaroos call a weekend cowboy, but in an arena he can outrope any buckaroo I ever saw. Jim gets off work at five, eats a quick supper, turns in the practice steers, his partner comes over, and they rope 30 head before the sun goes down. They do that three or four nights a week, then go to a jackpot roping on Saturday. While the buckaroo may rope 50 head all summer, Jim is roping a hundred head a week. Guess who is the better roper after a year or two?"

"So buckaroos don't go to the National Finals Rodeo,

the big one on television every December?'' Ella asked.

"Not unless they quit being buckaroos. The typical NFR roper, if there is such a thing, is a kid who was pretty good on the high school roping team, in a place like Oregon or North Dakota. Actually, more rodeo cowboys come from Texas and California than anywhere. After high school he gets a construction job earning $20 an hour, lives at home, saves every penny. In the fall, he borrows his dad's truck and trailer and heads to Arizona where there are practice arenas. He can pay to rope all winter. He gives his money to the arena owner, finds a partner, and starts roping, 50, 60, or 70 steers every day. On the weekends, he goes to jackpots. He finds a girlfriend who drives him around and gives him food because he doesn't have any money after he pays for his roping. That's how you become a national finals roper. But this isn't the national finals. Today we're having fun.''

"One of the mysteries of life," Ella said, "is why men think it is fun hurting things. I guess nobody here feels sorry for the poor steers.''

"Actually, roping is a big step above the more primitive sports, like hunting and bullfighting, where something has to die. I played football, and I know for a fact that roping steers sustain fewer injuries than football players. I just wish steers could talk.''

"So they could tell you what hurts?''

"So we could ask them some questions," Emmett continued. "I'd line them up against the fence and say, 'Everybody who wants to go back to Mexico where you nearly starved to death, raise your tail.' No tails would go up. Then I'd ask, 'Everybody who wants to go into one of those fancy feedlots where you sit around all day eating grain and silage so you can go to the slaughterhouse and get killed, raise your tail.' No tails would go up. Then I'd ask, 'How many want to stay here where you might get roped three or four times a week, but spend the rest of the time wandering around these beautiful hills, eating when you feel like it?' All the tails would go up.''

The Moriah Confession

"Let's rope!" Emmett yelled as he and Ella pushed the steers into the arena.

Emmett assigned Ella to a card table just outside the fence, where she began collecting entry fees and writing down the names of the teams in the first event, an open roping, meaning anyone could enter with anyone they wanted, regardless of age, skill level or sex. Emmett's partner was Billy Thunder.

While Ella was signing people up, Emmett went inside the arena to the roping chute to set up the barrier, an electric eye which turned on a light if the head horse came out of the box too soon. If the light went on, the team received a ten-second penalty.

Emmett was busy assembling the electric eye when Ella came to him, saying some new ropers had arrived and wanted to enter the open competition.

"Sign 'em up," Emmett said.

"They're different," she said.

"More buckaroos?"

"Beach bums, driving a black van with curtains on the windows. They are wearing cutoffs, no shirts, long hair, dark glasses. Say they are going to Florida to do a little surfing. They are pulling a two-horse trailer."

"Don't let them enter," Emmett said, playing with one of the wires to the electric eye. "Tell them they can stay for lunch. I'll give them some gas to get to Wendover, if they need it, but they can't rope with us."

"I don't understand, if they are willing to put up the entry fees ..."

"They're wuffs, that's why."

"My, how my vocabulary is growing," Ella said sarcastically. "Would you mind defining wuff?"

"Comes out of New Mexico. Probably a derivative of the word 'wolf.' Wuffs are professional ropers who are having a bad year. They know they are out of the running for the national finals, so instead of entering the big rodeos where entry fees are steep and the competition stiff, they go to ranch

90

rodeos like this to take the easy money from the weekend cowboys and buckaroos. The word gets out, so people won't let them enter, so they disguise themselves and show up as wuffs in sheep's clothing."

"They told me they were going to California to do some surfing, and I believed them," Ella said. "They have a surfboard tied to the top of their trailer."

"Go back and look at their saddles," Emmett said. "First look for duct tape covering up writing."

"What kind of writing?"

"Calgary Stampede, First Place, Cow Palace, Denver Stock Show, San Antonio Grand Champion Team Roper, things like that. If you find any words like those under the tape, you know they are wuffs. Then look at the swell on the right side of the header's saddle horn. See if it's worn. When a header turns a steer, the rope frequently rubs across the right swell."

"I'll be right back," Ella said, returning to her table and the two surfers. Five minutes later she returned to the chute, where Emmett was now satisfied that the electric eye was working properly.

"The heeler had tape on his saddle, just like you said," she explained. "When I asked him what the tape was covering up, he said the previous owner of the saddle had stamped his name on it, and since he didn't like the previous owner, he put tape over the name."

"Did you make him take the tape off?" Emmett asked.

"Yes. And I was embarrassed because he had been telling the truth. It didn't say Denver Stock Show or anything like that, just some old guy's name."

"What was the name?"

"It doesn't matter."

"Tell me the name."

"Bob Faust. No, Bob Feist."

"Did you find anything else?" Emmett asked, trying hard to suppress a smile.

"On the other saddle, the header's, a new piece of

leather was patched over the right swell.''

"You didn't sign them up, did you?''

"I told them I had to check with you.''

"They're wuffs. The Bob Feist is probably the most prestigious roping in the world. Costs a thousand dollars a man to enter. The winning team walks away with $100,000 in winnings. Anyone who can win a saddle at Bob Feist doesn't belong here. Did you get their names?''

"Zane and Jim.''

"I think I know who they are. They could tie three of these steers in 15 seconds. Tell them to stay and have lunch before they head out to California.''

The ropers were in the arena now, galloping in a counterclockwise circle, warming up their horses. Some were swinging ropes as they galloped along.

Ella was assigned the task of keeping time. She was to start the stopwatch when the gate opened to let the steer out, then stop the clock when the judge's flag went down. If he said, "Plus five,'' she was to add a five-second penalty because the heeler had caught only one foot. If someone at the chute yelled "Breakout'' or "Barrier violation,'' she was to add ten seconds, the penalty for the head horse coming out too soon.

Another woman, who introduced herself as Claire, was on the loudspeaker, announcing whose turn it was to rope, which team was on deck, and who should be ready to be on deck. She used first names only.

"Ropers, clear the arena,'' Claire announced, when it was time to begin.

Before the first team entered the box, Emmett rode over to Claire and borrowed her microphone. He made an announcement, mentioning an incident in Colorado in which a roper had caught his foot in the stirrup while falling from his horse. Someone had left the arena gate open. The horse had run out of the arena and down the road, dragging the roper until he was dead.

"Don't want that happening on the Medicine Springs

Chapter 8

Ranch," Emmett said. "Please keep the arena gates closed."
Several times during the course of the day Emmett made the
same announcement. The ropers seemed to have a hard time
remembering his admonition. Twice during the roping, when
her services weren't needed at the scoring table, Ella walked
over to the gate and closed it so Emmett wouldn't have to
make another announcement.

Emmett and Billy were the third team to rope. Ella
watched closely as Emmett and Geronimo entered the header's
box and turned around. The horse was at the back of the box,
on the far side, facing out into the arena. Geronimo was
standing perfectly still, his weight equally balanced on his four
powerful legs. His head was high, his ears forward, his lower
lip quivering, his eyes on fire. Ella had never seen a horse
look more alert, more beautiful.

Emmett was leaning forward in the saddle, a slight arch
in his back. In his left hand were three coils of rope and
Geronimo's reins. In his right hand was the loop, which
looked too small, but Ella knew he would feed more rope into
the loop as he started swinging.

Emmett checked to make sure Billy was ready, then
nodded, the black brim of his hat making a quick dip. The
gate clanked open, and Ella started the stopwatch. A tan steer
charged into the arena. An instant later, the two ropers raced
out of their respective boxes. Emmett was leaning forward,
standing in his stirrups, vigorously swinging his rope.
Geronimo was accelerating to top speed, rapidly gaining on
the steer, the horse's huge muscles exploding, his ears back
flat against his head like he was attacking the steer.

Billy Thunder was racing at full gallop on the right side
of the steer. His right hand was extended out and up, holding
a big loop. He had not yet begun to swing it over his head.

Geronimo was just catching up to the steer when
Emmett threw his loop. It caught the right horn, rolling over
the left one, the slack rolling around to the left, forming a
figure-eight. Emmett's right hand moved back behind his
knee, pulling the rope tight. As he was doing this, Geronimo

began to slow down. As soon as the loop was tight around the steer's horns, Emmett's right hand shot to the saddle horn, making a quick dally. As he did so, the rope jerked the steer's head up and back. Geronimo dug in hard with his front feet and made a ninety-degree turn to the left, maintaining his speed while doing so. The steer turned, too, flip-flopping while turning the corner but quickly straightening out as the horse pulled him along.

No sooner had the steer made the turn than Billy was close on its left hip, his big loop swinging briskly in a dipping motion over his horse's head. After the steer made its second hop, Billy guided his big loop under its belly as both hind feet entered the loop. Billy's right hand shot high in the air as his horse sat down and slid to a halt, both actions jerking the loop tight before the steer could hop out of it.

An instant later the flag went down. Ella pushed the button on the stopwatch and looked down. The time was 7.3 seconds, the best so far.

She wrote down the time, then watched Emmett gallop to the end of the arena to remove his rope from the steer. She thought that whoever told her team roping was boring didn't know what they were talking about. This was exciting. She tried to imagine Emmett's excitement, feeling the speed and power of the horse charging from the box, the thrill of making a ninety-degree turn at a full gallop with a wild steer on the end of the rope. There would be a lot of satisfaction in making a successful run, with so much speed, power, balance, skill and timing involved. Ella's heart was pounding, and she guessed Emmett's was, too. This sure beat the socks off of watching a football scrimmage.

Each team had three opportunities to catch steers in the open roping. When it was over, Emmett and Billy had captured second place, with winnings of about $90. Winnings comprised two-thirds of the entry fees. The other third went to the producer, who provided the facility, the cattle, the management, and in this case, the lunch. Ella learned this was standard procedure at ropings everywhere.

Chapter 8

The only unfortunate incident during the first roping occurred when a roper from Delta, after missing his steer, began whipping and spurring his horse. As he came past Ella's scoring table, Billy Thunder spoke up. "Why don't you beat your hand instead of your horse?" Billy was suggesting that the roper, not the horse, was responsible for the miss. The roper offered no rebuttal as he disappeared behind the chute.

After the open competition, everyone stopped for lunch. Someone had started the barbecue grill, and Emmett provided all the fixings for hamburgers. Everything else was potluck. Salads, bags of chips, cases of beer and pop, even an ice chest full of ice cream bars, showed up at the old picnic table. Some of the people went down by the stream to eat on the grass, others up by the pond. Some stayed by the table.

After a quick bite, Emmett and some of the ropers got involved in an intense discussion on the upcoming afternoon roping activities. There was going to be a mixed roping where one of the partners had to be over 50, a woman, or under 18. Some of the men wanted to make it under 17, so Billy couldn't rope with Emmett.

Emmett finally conceded. Then the discussion became more heated as some of the men tried to pair up Wade Hanks with an old sheepherder from Gandy.

Ella decided to go for a walk, to the top of the little hill across the road from the bunkhouse. From the top, she would be able to see the arena with the horses and steers on her left, the house and yard on her right, the sprawling meadows of the Medicine Springs Ranch and Deep Creek Mountains directly in front of her. The view would be fabulous, she thought.

She was about halfway up the hill when Emmett came galloping up on Geronimo. Her first thought was that something was wrong. Emmett was laughing, but it seemed like a forced laugh. He seemed nervous.

"Come back with me and have some ice cream," he said.

"I'm not hungry," Ella said easily. "I just thought I'd

95

walk to the top of the hill, look around a bit. I'll come down when the roping starts."

"I want you to come with me now and have some ice cream," Emmett said, his voice more forceful. She couldn't figure out what was wrong.

"Bring the ice cream up here," she said. "We can eat together, on top of the hill."

"No. I have to go back. And you have to come with me."

Emmett moved the horse sideways, just downhill from Ella. Then he removed his foot from the stirrup, telling her to put her foot in the stirrup and swing up behind him. Reluctantly, she did so. She placed one hand on each side of his waist for balance.

As the horse started down the hill, Emmett leaned back, his muscular shoulders brushing gently against her breasts. She did not pull away.

As they entered the yard, her heart was pounding, but not only from being physically close to Emmett. There was a new mystery concerning Emmett Hays. There was something on the hill he did not want her to see. It was almost like he was frightened to have her go up there, but what could it be? She would find out when Emmett was not around. But how and when?

In the mixed roping, Emmett paired up with a lady named Julie from Callao. She said she was a grandmother, but looked much younger. She and Emmett won the third place money.

The final roping of the day was called a Mormon roping—an event where the header catches the steer on horseback, but the heeler has to do his part on foot.

"Why do they call it a Mormon roping?" Ella asked Emmett.

"I'm not sure, except that it originated in Arizona," he explained. "Supposedly, there was a roping where two Mormons showed up to compete, but only had one horse between them. Some say they brought only one horse because

96

Chapter 8

they were stupid. Others say it was because they were poor. At any rate, the header rode the horse, and the heeler roped on foot. What they did became an event known as a Mormon roping. The heeler can get pretty winded if the header doesn't catch in a hurry.''

"Seems like Mormons might be offended,'' Ella said.

"No. Most of the folks here are Mormons, some not very good ones, but nobody has complained. I guess if we called it a Black, Mexican or Jewish roping, there'd be some complaints.''

"Who will be your partner?'' she asked.

"Billy Thunder. That's why he wore his sneakers. He's no buckaroo. He's the fastest runner in these parts, and wants to win this one bad. We ought to do it if I don't miss the heads.''

After Emmett and Billy won the Mormon roping, everybody started loading their horses in the trailers and leaving. It had been a great day—good weather, no accidents, and lots of fun.

"When do you have to go?'' Emmett asked Ella, as the last truck pulled out of the yard.

"I have commitments in Spanish Fork in the morning, so I have to go back tonight,'' she said.

"There's still a couple of hours of daylight, if you would like to see some wild horses,'' he said. "There's something else I'd like to show you, too.''

"Like whatever it was you were trying to keep me from on top of the hill,'' Ella said, looking directly into his intense, gray eyes.

"Someday, I'll show you, but not today. Can you live with that?''

"Sure,'' she said. "Let's see the wild horses.'' They got in his truck and headed towards the valley.

Chapter 9

Emmett drove a few miles down the road. He pulled the truck off on the right shoulder as he brought it to a stop, then turned off the engine.

"Let's walk from here," he said, getting out of the truck.

Ella was about to ask Emmett if he was going to take the keys out of the ignition, roll up his window, and lock the door, then decided not to. Then as an afterthought, she asked if he ever took the keys out of his truck and locked it.

"Just when I go to the big city," he answered. "Never out here."

Emmett and Ella walked side by side up a jeep trail, winding through tall sagebrush. Several cows were ahead of them, following the same trail.

"I thought cows ate grass," Ella said.

"They do."

"I can't see any grass, but the cows look healthy.

Where does the grass grow, besides the meadows around the house?"

"It grows up high in the mountains where we take the cattle in the summer. And there are pockets of grass on this desert winter range, but the cows eat a lot of other things, too. Tell me what you see around us."

"Sagebrush, and lots of it," she observed.

"The experienced eye sees a lot more than sagebrush," Emmett explained. "Actually there are about eight kinds of brush, and four or five varieties are nourishing to the cattle."

Wandering off the trail, Emmett showed Ella some white sage, explaining that it was the best winter feed of all because of its 35 percent protein content. He showed her greasewood and bud sage which the cattle loved in the spring. He pointed out shad scale and Brigham tea. He showed her why ranchers didn't need to put out salt on this kind of range, because the cows got all they needed from several kinds of plants.

"With all this stuff to eat," Emmett concluded, "it doesn't matter if there is any grass. Sometimes when I watch a cow eating, she'll walk right past the grass to get at the plants I just showed you. Cows raised in this country do best because they learn at an early age what to eat. Cows brought in from outside, who are used to grass-filled pastures, sometimes have a hard time adapting. Mine did when I brought them here from Wyoming."

"Where are we going?" she asked.

"To a spring frequented by wild horses," Emmett said. "And I'll bet you can't guess what it is called."

"I'm sure I can't," she said. "Unless you want to give me a hint."

"It's named after someone close to you," he said teasingly.

"George?" she guessed.

"I thought you two were not very close," Emmett said, not caring for her answer.

"We aren't during the football season, that's for sure."

Chapter 9

"Starts with an E," Emmett said, wanting to change the subject.

"Emmett?"

"No, Ella Spring. It's named after you."

"No it isn't."

"It really is Ella Spring," he insisted.

"Who is the Ella it is named after?" she asked.

"Obviously a woman. Maybe she lived around here. Maybe she was the girlfriend of the person who named the spring. Perhaps he had a premonition that someday you would come here, that you would be very beautiful, so he named the place after you."

"I doubt that," Ella said, enjoying the flattery, feeling a little embarrassed, and knowing Emmett should not be saying things like that to her. "But you're not kidding me. It is really called Ella Spring?"

"Yes," he said, his voice suddenly very soft, almost a whisper. He held his finger against his lips, a signal for her to be quiet, too.

She followed him off the trail, through the tall brush, up a little hill. Directly in front of them on the side of the hill was a half circle of neatly piled rocks. The area inside was dug down a foot or two.

"An Indian hunting blind," he whispered, as they stepped inside and dropped to their knees. "The Native Americans built this, probably hundreds of years ago, so they could hide in here, out of sight of the game animals coming to water—antelope, deer, bighorn sheep, and wild horses, like the ones we are looking for today."

Ella looked through a notch in the wall. She could see a little pond about 50 yards down the hill and up the draw. Two or three springs fed into the pond. The new grass around the pond and springs had been cropped close by animals. Piles of horse manure were everywhere.

In the middle of the Jeep trail which passed close by the pond and springs, Ella saw two huge piles of horse droppings, perhaps ten times as big as the others she had seen.

"If I didn't know better, I'd swear you had elephants around here," she whispered. "Why are those two piles in the road so much bigger than the others?"

"Stud piles," he said. "A stallion with mares will do his business in the same place day after day. It's a territorial marker, a warning to other stallions to stay away if they don't want to get beat up."

"Does the size of the pile mean anything?" Ella asked. "Do the more dominant stallions make bigger piles?"

"I don't think so. The size of the pile is more a function of how much the stud has been eating and how often he comes to water here."

"You suggested last week that I might want to write a paper on wild horses. What exactly did you have in mind?"

"Remember the book *Unsafe at any Speed*, by Ralph Nader?"

"General Motors stopped producing the Corvair because of the book," Ella said.

"A book like that could be written on wild horse management. I've thought of doing it myself. Maybe I will someday. Did you see the movie *Misfits*, with Clark Gable and Marilyn Monroe?"

"You're kidding. That movie was old when I was in junior high school. But I think I saw it. Marilyn drove the truck across the salt flats after the wild horses. Gable stood in the back and roped the mustangs. The ropes were tied to big tires which the horses dragged around until all the fight was out of them."

"You have a good memory," he said. "During the forties and fifties there were a lot of people who did that. They were called mustangers. They sold the horses for dog food and mink food. Ranchers, more often than not, just shot the wild horses to prevent them from competing with cattle for feed. With no one to watch out for them, the point finally came where wild horses were facing extinction."

"Enter Wild Horse Annie," Ella said, vaguely remembering some things she had read in newspapers and magazines as a little girl.

"Right. Annie comes along, stirs up a lot of interest and support for wild horses. She did a lot more than anyone ever thought she would. She got Congress to pass an act to save the wild horses, The Wild Horse Act. While almost everyone agrees it was a good idea to save the mustangs, the law didn't adequately provide for the management of future wild horse herds.

"Under the new law no one could chase and catch mustangs. No one could sell them. No one could shoot wild horses. The result was that the mustangs began to multiply and replenish the western deserts, and soon became more numerous than they had been before. No longer facing extinction, the growing herds began to destroy fragile desert habitat and create a whole new set of problems for farmers and stockmen.

"So the government began catching horses in areas where they had become too numerous, and put them up for adoption. For the most part, the ranchers and cowboys who knew what the horses were and what it takes to break them didn't want them, so the government took them to the cities, mostly in the East, where many people's experience in handling wild horses was limited to what they had learned in the *Black Beauty* and *My Friend Flicka* movies."

"How could the government assume that people not experienced in riding and handling horses would find success with mustangs?" she asked.

"They published a little booklet telling people how to do it. I would like to see an independent study showing how many adopted mustangs actually become usable horses."

"And how many owners of the other ones sustained injuries," she added.

"Adopting a five-year-old wild stallion for your teenage daughter who has never handled a horse before would be riskier than sending her on a blind date with boxer Mike Tyson," Emmett said.

"At least they found a way to get rid of the excess

horses," Ella said.

"Not exactly. If someone is willing to pay a hundred dollars to adopt a horse, they want a young and pretty one. Most of the horses available for adoption are not young and pretty."

"So what happens to the horses no one wants?" Ella asked.

"They lock them away in feedlots, spending millions of dollars every year feeding them, after the government has already spent $700 each rounding them up."

"Maybe that's a small price to pay to save the mustangs," Ella speculated. "Do you have a better idea?"

"Absolutely. Turn the management of the mustang over to the wildlife experts, the fish and game departments in each state. Let the wildlife biologists monitor the herds and determine how many animals need to be removed each year to maintain the most desirable population. Then let the respective wildlife agencies have a draw and sell permits, as they do with elk, deer, antelope and bighorn sheep. The revenue from the sale of the permits would fund the management programs for the mustangs. Instead of being a drain on the taxpayer, the mustang could pay its own way, even generate wildlife revenues for the states.

"A new sport would be born, with its own season, probably in the fall, and rules of fair chase. No airplanes, motorized vehicles or firearms. Only saddle horses and ropes, the way it was done a hundred years ago. With more people enjoying the resource, the long-term survival of the species would be assured."

"But permit holders would only want the young and beautiful animals," she said.

"Deer and elk hunters want trophy animals, but knowing the season will be over in three days, two weeks, or whatever, they take what they can get. It will be the same way with mustang chasers. It is better to come home with a marginal horse than none at all. Let the free market determine the fate of the captured mustangs. The young and beautiful animals will end up in the stalls and pastures of those who catch them. The marginal animals will end up on the dinner tables of France, where they should be going now.''

"And you think I ought to write about this?'' she asked.

"It would be a big deal,'' he said. "You would have to get a congressman involved, probably one from Nevada or Wyoming, who would be willing to sponsor legislation to amend The Wild Horse Act. You could be on every talk show, have a write-up on the front page of every newspaper.''

"Would you help me?'' Ella asked.

"Sure, but lets not decide tonight. Think about it for a week or two. In the meantime, I'll give you some things to read.''

"I have never even seen a mustang,'' she said.

"Hopefully we can take care of that tonight,'' Emmett said. They continued to watch the spring, and the hills beyond, but no wild horses appeared.

"I'm sure you've heard of some of the polygamist groups who settle in this remote west desert country,'' he said.

"Yes. I've seen some television news coverage.''

"Some are humans, but most are horses,'' he said. "Wild horses are the ultimate polygamists. When you see a herd of mustangs, like the ones using this spring, there is one stallion; all the rest are mares and foals. No exceptions. When you see a single horse, or groups of two or three, they are bachelor stallions—the ones too old, too young, too weak or too dumb to get and keep their own harem of mares. There are no single females.

"In wild horses you see an accelerated form of Darwin's process of natural selection. Only the strong, smart and dominant herd stallions do the breeding. If a bachelor stallion wants to breed a mare, first he must defeat the herd stallion and take his place. Every year, as the herd stallion gets older, the young bachelor stallions get stronger, and battles of dominance take place. When the herd stallion is finally defeated—and because of old age, that day always comes—he loses his mares and will father no more foals."

"It seems sad that he must leave his wives and children," she added.

"Yes and no," he said. "After a couple of years, a stallion will have an increasing number of his own daughters in his harem, resulting in inbreeding, a force pushing the natural selection process in the negative direction. When the old stallion is defeated, the new stallion brings in a new gene pool, resulting in hybrid vigor. It's too bad Darwin couldn't have observed the wild horses of the western United States before writing *Origin of the Species.*"

"But there doesn't appear to be a selective process taking place on the female side," Ella added. "Only the best and strongest males are allowed to breed, but all the females are having foals."

"Not all, and not all with the same frequency," he explained. "Females, human and animal, have this thing we call the biological clock, which not only counts the days until menopause but controls, or at least influences, ovulation cycles. I've read where Jewish women in Nazi concentration camps during World War II frequently stopped having their periods. Their biological clocks told their bodies it would not be wise to have a baby in a concentration camp. Their bodies responded by stopping the ovulation process.

"When I brought my herd of cattle to this desert country from Wyoming, they found themselves in strange surroundings with scarce water and different kinds of plants to learn to eat. A local rancher told me I would make the Cowboy Hall of Fame if more than 60 percent of my cows conceived the first year. The normal conception rate for a herd like mine is over 90 percent. He was telling me that the biological clock in each of those cows was saying, 'Hey, let's stop ovulating until we know whether or not we'll survive in this strange new environment.' My conception rate that first year was about 75 percent. The second year it went to 85 percent, and was normal by the third season.

"Mustang mares have biological clocks, too. If a mare

is healthy and strong, and socially content near the top of the pecking order, she cycles regularly. On the other hand, a mare at the bottom of the social structure, on the fringe of the herd, perhaps because she is smaller, weaker, or dumber than the others, has a biological clock telling her her situation is at best precarious, and maybe it wouldn't be a good idea to get pregnant. While the superior mare might have eight or ten foals in a lifetime, the marginal mare may have only one or two foals, or none at all. The biological clock can control the females very dramatically in the natural selection process."

"I've never given much thought to Darwin, or taken his theories very seriously," Ella added. Through the dip in the rock wall, they were still watching the water hole and the hills beyond, quietly conversing as they waited for wild horses to come to water.

"I shouldn't either," Emmett said. "When you apply what he said to wild horses, his theories make a lot of sense, but when you try to apply them to the human race, it gets kind of frightening."

"Why's that?"

"I don't know how you could measure it, but it appears the poor, weak and lazy males might be doing a lot more breeding than the more successful males in our society. Men at the lower end of the social order seem to father more children than the males at the upper end. Someone ought to do a study to find out if welfare bums are fathering more children than Harvard graduates. It appears they are. King Solomon had seven hundred wives and probably as many children. Bill Clinton has Hillary, and she isn't popping out the offspring with any degree of regularity—and maybe that's a good thing.

"Of course, our government is making the situation even worse by giving financial incentives to those at the bottom of the social order to have more children, in the form of larger welfare checks. If Darwin's theories are correct, the human race, at least in this country, could be breeding itself to new lows, instead of new highs.

"The exception might be in the polygamist societies of

Utah's deserts and mountains," Emmett added.

"Now you've gone too far," Ella said. "You can't tell me a religious kook who runs off to the desert to wait for the end of the world, dragging a handful of helpless, deluded women with him, is pulling the human race up by its bootstraps."

"Like most people in mainstream, urban society, you have an oversimplified, cliched concept of the polygamous societies that are quietly filling the land," Emmett countered.

"You know all about it, a man who doesn't even have a single wife," Ella observed.

"The polygamists are more like the wild horses than you realize," he said, ignoring her stinging comment.

"Over the years," he continued, "I've known a number of bachelor polygamists—typically a man who decides for religious or other reasons that he ought to have plural wives. He tells his first wife what he intends to do. She divorces him, but he is unsuccessful in convincing other women to marry him, thus he joins the ranks of bachelor polygamists. He becomes one of the bachelor stallions, like those two coming down the hill over there."

Ella looked where Emmett was pointing. Two horses, a black with a white snip on his nose and a bay, were working their way down to water. They didn't seem to be in any hurry to get there, nor did they seem to be particularly cautious.

"They're young stallions," Emmett whispered.

"How do you know?" she asked.

"Not all scarred and beaten up. Too sleek and fat. They are just coming into their prime. The black one looks like he's ready to challenge the herd stallion, maybe this year."

"I didn't think stallions were friendly with each other," she said, barely whispering so the horses couldn't hear her. "These two look like best friends."

"They are, but turn a mare in with them, and they'll fight to the death over her. Take the mare away and they will be friends again."

"They are like people, aren't they?"

Chapter 9

"They are like the polygamists, in that the best men are fathering the most children. The man who can provide an adequate living, control his temper, be kind, loving and nurturing to his wives and children, maintain balance and harmony in a household with several women, seems to attract more wives, and keep the biological clocks ticking on the ones he's got."

By now the horses had reached the water and were drinking, first the black, then the bay. When finished, they held their heads high, looking around, clear water dripping from their mouths. The sun dropped behind the mountain as they turned from the water to head back up the mountain.

"They're beautiful," Ella whispered.

"Yes, but they are not content, and they never will be until they have herds of their own. That is the purpose of their existence, and they will not be happy until they have achieved that purpose. And when they get their own herds, they will have to fight battles every day to keep their herds together. Their moments in the sun will be short, and glorious, then they will have to step down." No more horses came to water.

"It's getting late," Ella said. "I have a long drive ahead of me." They stood up and started towards the truck.

"I'd sure like to know why you are so protective of your personal life," she said as they were walking down the Jeep trail to the main road.

"Maybe I'm afraid I will scare you away."

"Are your secrets that dark and sinister?" she asked.

"They are not sinister, and they are not dark. But they have brought me much pain. Taking care of cows, hard work, and roping have been my painkillers, my butte."

"You don't think talking about your wounds would help heal them?" she asked.

"Perhaps, but just having you here has been a healing influence. Another good thing was a pack trip I took to the Moriah wilderness, not long after the car wreck. Would you like to go there with me?"

"I would like that," Ella said quickly, "but I won't."

109

"I can't persuade you to come back?"

"No. With what the Army sent me, what you have shown me, and what the Indians told me, I have enough material for my massacre article. I will send you a copy, but I will not be back."

"You're not interested in doing the other articles we talked about, the one on the mustangs, and the photo piece on the Moriah wilderness?" Emmett asked.

"The problem is I am too interested, not just in the articles, but in you. I won't be coming back."

"You don't want to know why I was excommunicated?"

"I'm married to George Tanner."

"I don't think I have been too familiar, too friendly."

"You haven't done anything wrong. I just can't keep coming out here to see you. That's all. This is the last time."

They walked in silence for a minute, finally reaching the truck. It was almost dark. A warm April breeze was moving gently up the canyon from the desert. A full moon was just beginning to show its face over the eastern hills.

"Can we stay in touch?" he asked. "Letters, phone calls. If I come to a roping in Spanish Fork, maybe you would come and watch, or I could buy you a hamburger."

"Perhaps ... no, we have to end it here," Ella answered, her voice breaking.

"Look at me," he said, turning to face her. She looked up into his eyes, knowing she shouldn't. She hoped in the partial darkness he wouldn't see the tears beginning to spill out of the corners of hers.

"Have you ever had the feeling that our coming together was somehow right?" he asked. "Haven't you felt it was more than coincidence that I knew you were from Spanish Fork and had two children?"

"I don't want to talk about it. I have to go." The tears were streaming down Ella's cheeks as she started to turn away. But he wouldn't let her. He placed his hands on her shoulders and pulled her to him. She knew she should resist,

110

but couldn't as his strong arms encircled her. She buried her head against his muscular chest. The scent of horse sweat and dust was wonderful.

Ella could feel Emmett's lips gently kissing the top of her head. She wanted to raise her face to his and press her lips to his. Instead, she fought for control, continuing to press the side of her head against his chest. She could feel him kissing her forehead now. Oh, how she wanted to give in, but she must not. Mustering all her strength, Ella pushed him away, walked around to the passenger side of the truck, and got in. They drove back to the ranch in silence.

As soon as the truck was stopped, she ran to the bunk house, grabbed her things, and threw them in the Jeep. Emmett walked up to Ella as she started to get in.

"Please come back," he said. This time there were tears in his eyes.

"If I do, will you show me what's on top of the hill? Will you tell me what apostasy means?"

"When I take you to the top of the hill, you will know everything," he said.

Ella realized she had to leave before all her resistance caved in. She got in the Jeep, started the engine, said goodby to Emmett, and roared out of the yard and down the road, believing she would never come back to the Medicine Springs Ranch, not ever. When she passed the turnoff to Ella Spring, tears began streaming down her cheeks for the second time that night.

Chapter 10

Ella didn't go back the next week, or the week after that. With the school year winding down, there was a lot going on at work, and at home. That helped. She finished her article on the Goshute massacre and sent it to a quarterly historical publication.

The news one night featured a sheepherder who stormed the BLM regional office in Fillmore, carrying a loaded gun and threatening to shoot people. There was footage of the herder voicing his complaint, standing by his herd in the west desert. The mountain in the background looked like Moriah. Ella had a deep, aching feeling in her chest and stomach that lasted all night, preventing her from sleeping.

A week later, a television station did a feature on the upcoming graduating class of five at the West Desert School.

"How would you like to go to a school like that?" Ella asked Kevin and Laura, who were in the room watching television with her.

"I bet I could start on the basketball team," Kevin said.

"I'd probably graduate with honors," Laura, the good student, responded.

The aching feeling returned. Ella decided to stop watching the news.

A few days later, the mailman delivered a large brown envelope with a Wendover postmark. There was no name with the return address, but she knew when it said Star Route, Pleasant Valley, the envelope had to be from Emmett. She held it close to her chest as she ran down the hall to her bedroom and closed the door.

The package contained brochures and booklets on wild horses. Emmett had marked some of the parts with a yellow felt-tip marker. Frantically, Ella thumbed through the pages, hoping there might be a note of some kind. There was not. She kept the brochures by her bed.

A week later, she received another envelope from Wendover. This one contained a BLM brochure on the Moriah wilderness, and a letter from Emmett.

Dear Ella:

Number 53 had a healthy bull calf. No problems. The calving is just about finished. Billy Thunder got his big one. The tribe rejected his proposal. He took off. Nobody knows where he went, but I guess with $50,000 in his pocket he won't starve.

I'd hold another roping if I thought you would help. No one has ridden Tithing since you left. The snow is rapidly melting on Moriah. Soon, we'll be able to ride up there. Lots of moisture. The wildflowers and bristlecones will be fabulous. Have you thought any more about doing an article?

Occasionally, I stop by Ella Spring, remembering the time we spent there, wishing I had more than just a spring named Ella around here.

Emmett

Chapter 10

Ella read the letter five times, stuffed it in the bottom of her purse, and had another sleepless night. At 4 a.m. she got out of bed and finished off the last of the candy she had picked up at the mall during her shopping spree. She felt angry at Emmett for the way he had turned her life inside out.

The next morning, upon returning to her office after her ten o'clock class, Ella found a message to call Harriet.

"What's new in the alumni business?" Ella asked when Harriet came on the phone.

"Segment marketing," Harriet responded. "It's not enough anymore just to have an alumni list. Now the names have to be broken down into what they call market segments. And that's why I called you."

"Why would an English teacher be interested in market segments?"

"Because one of them includes the names of BYU graduates who went to prestigious schools to earn advanced degrees—schools like Oxford, Stanford, Princeton, Harvard, Yale, and Columbia. Guess where Mr. Emmett Hays went to graduate school."

"I couldn't begin to guess."

"You spent a whole weekend with him, and he never told you where he did his graduate work? Nobody is that modest."

"Where did he go?"

"Harvard."

"Probably a mistake. You're confusing him with someone else."

"We use Social Security numbers to cross reference. There's no mistake. Emmett Hays, the west desert cowboy, is a Harvard man."

Ella found herself reaching into the bottom of her purse and pulling out the letter.

"Did you ever find out why he was excommunicated?" Harriet asked.

"No. But he said if I would walk with him to the top of a little hill near the ranch house, I would know why."

"What's on the hill?"

"I don't know. I didn't go up there."

"You're not curious?"

"I'm very curious. Things just didn't work out to enable me to go up there."

"I'll go with you, if you want to, some night and sneak up on the hill while Emmett is sleeping. When do you want to go?"

"I couldn't do that behind his back."

"OK, I'll let you know if I find anything else. Goodby."

That evening, after supper, after the children had gone to a church activity, Ella and George had a fight. Ella didn't know what prompted him to bring up the subject, but he said something about being the only man in the athletic department whose wife didn't care if the teams won or lost.

"You wouldn't care if they shut down the whole football program," he complained.

"You're wrong," Ella said, sarcasm in her voice. "I would care. I would be glad they did. I am sick of all the broadcasts and re-broadcasts. It would be wonderful to get Paul James and Jay Monson out of my living room and bedroom."

"You really mean that, don't you?" he whined.

"Do you think my feelings are grounds for divorce?" she asked, as surprised at what she was saying as George was.

"I wouldn't quit my job to keep this marriage together, if that's what you want," he said.

"I wouldn't want you to quit the work you love," Ella said, her voice softer. "I was just wondering if the differences between you and me are too great to justify keeping this marriage together. That's all."

"That's all! A divorce would ruin my career at BYU, and yours, too."

"A lot of people at BYU are divorced."

"It carries a stigma."

"If all you're worried about is careers and stigma,

maybe we should go ahead and do it,'' she challenged.

"Maybe we should," George said, anger in his voice. "Maybe I could find someone more interested in going to Cougar Stadium on Saturday afternoons than wandering around the desert wondering if somebody's old cow had eaten too much greasewood."

Ella was surprised George remembered anything she had told him about her trip to the west desert. Without another word, he turned and stomped out of the house, slamming the door behind him. She picked up the phone and dialed Emmett's number.

"George and I just had a big fight. We're talking about divorce," she began, not wanting to spend a lot of time on the unimportant things. "I want to know where you stand with the Church. You have that horrible slot machine in your living room. You sponsor a Mormon roping, which is a put-down. You've been excommunicated. The Church is important to me. I want to know where you stand."

"Whoa. You're going too fast. You caught me by surprise," Emmett said. "It sounds like you want a testimony meeting on the telephone."

"That would do, for starters."

"OK. I was raised in the Church. Grew up on my parent's ranch in Star Valley, Wyoming. That's where I learned about cows, and how to rope. Played football in high school. Went on a mission to Mexico, baptized 23 people. Finished my degree at BYU while playing football."

"What about the Church?" she asked. "How do you feel about it now?"

"I remember as a boy feeling like my whole body was full of fire when President Kimball talked in general conference. Sometimes I would get the same feeling when I read the scriptures, also when I would fast and pray about something important. I believe the Church is true, as much now as ever. I think I have what I think you would consider a strong testimony."

"But?" she asked.

117

"I don't have any real problems with the doctrine, but there are a few things I don't understand about administrative matters," he said. "Nothing serious."

"Like what?"

"I don't understand why a church that believes in revelation uses seniority, instead of revelation, to pick its prophet, seer and revelator. Especially when the seniority system doesn't seem to be working. I mean, what would happen to General Motors if the corporate officer who had been there the longest automatically became the president?"

"The Church isn't General Motors," Ella countered, "and from where I stand, the Church doesn't seem to be running amok with the present system of selecting leaders. Maybe old men are wiser than the young, energetic guys you would like to see at the helm."

"Forget the young, energetic guys. How about a seasoned, time-tested, silver-haired spiritual leader in his late sixties or seventies? When Moses got old he turned the reins over to Aaron and wandered off in the desert to die. When King Benjamin got old, he gave his farewell address and turned over the keys to Alma. Why can't church leaders do that today?"

"I don't know," she said. "But I do know you have an attitude problem, and until you get it straightened out it's going to be a long time before you find your way back into the Church. What else bothers you?"

"I wish the Church would be nicer to polygamists. I see a lot of them out here. Basically, they are pretty good people who believe polygamy is part of the gospel—and it is, historically and doctrinally. Maybe the Church should work with these people instead of excommunicating them."

"By allowing these people in the Church," Ella responded, "it would essentially be accepting, or re-introducing, polygamy."

"The history and doctrine would support such a move," Emmett added.

"Emmett, would you like my honest assessment of what

you are saying?'' she asked.

"Sure.''

"When it comes to selecting a prophet, you tell me the Church should abandon tradition and rely on revelation.''

"That's right.''

"On the other hand, in dealing with polygamy, you say the Church should ignore the revelations of its present leaders and rely on tradition. Should the Church rely on tradition or revelation? Whichever way the Church is leaning, you think the other way is better. The real problem here isn't Church administration, but the critical attitude of Emmett Hays. Like Dale Carnegie said, 'Any fool can criticize, condemn and complain, and most fools do.' ''

"I've been called a fool before, but never so nicely,'' Emmett said.

"But we're still beating around the bush, Emmett,'' she observed. "The purpose of this phone call isn't to resolve conflicts in church administration, or to provide attitude therapy for Emmett Hays.''

"What, then, is the purpose of this conversation?'' he asked.

"Let's just say I'm exploring possibilities,'' Ella responded. She hesitated. Maybe she would be better off listening to Paul James and Jay Monson, instead of opening the door to the kinds of issues that concerned Emmett Hays. And she still wasn't to the bottom of it.

"What's on the hill?'' she asked.

"My Gethsemane,'' he said. "If you come out, I will show you. After you see it, you may never want to speak to Emmett Hays again. I will not discuss it on the phone.''

"Do you think you could love me?'' Ella asked impulsively.

"I already do, more than you will ever know, but there's the hill. Please come out again.''

"I'll call again, in a few days. Goodby.'' She hung up the phone, and prepared to suffer through another sleepless night. She decided to buy some more candy. And it was time for another shopping spree at the mall.

Chapter 11

Several times during the night Ella slipped out of bed and prayed about her situation with Emmett. She knew if she asked anyone about it, particularly George or the bishop, they would tell her it was absolutely wrong for her to go out there again, or to pursue the relationship any further. Yet, she had a strong feeling that she and Emmett were supposed to meet, that destiny had brought them together, that there was a higher or hidden purpose behind what was happening, and that it was not finished.

Perhaps she was supposed to play a role in helping Emmett resolve a deep problem related to the mystery on the hill. Maybe she was supposed to divorce George and marry Emmett. Things like that happened all the time. She knew a number of people whose second marriages seemed made in heaven. On this particular night, she begged the Lord to give her a sign that she might know what to do.

The next morning Ella stopped by the *Herald* in

Springville to pick up some printing for one of her classes. While waiting for her job to get trimmed and wrapped, she chatted with Martin, the publisher, whom she had known for many years. When she mentioned she had been out in the west desert doing research on an Indian massacre, he said that with summer coming he wished he could get someone to go out there and do a photo piece for several of his newspapers on the new Moriah wilderness.

"Would you like me to do it?" she asked, her hands getting clammy as she remembered her earnest prayer requesting a sign. "I'm pretty good with a camera, and a local rancher has offered to show me the way onto the Moriah table where he says most of the wildlife hangs out. He said he knows some fabulous photo locations."

"Is there any chance you could do it in the next few weeks?" Martin asked.

"I think so," Ella said, glad he couldn't put a stethoscope on her chest and hear the wild pounding of her heart.

On the way to school, she felt more than a little foolish at how physical her reaction had been to the possibility of doing the Moriah piece. Was this the sign she had been praying for, or was the assignment merely a coincidence?

"Lord, please give me another sign," she begged, momentarily closing her eyes as she drove over the Ironton Hill.

After her one o'clock class, Ella stopped by the Alumni House to see Harriet. There had been no further communication with Harriet since finding out about Emmett going to Harvard.

"Nothing else on the mysterious cowboy," Harriet said. "I checked the list of graduates who have held top executive positions with major corporations—Black and Decker, General Mills, Ford, and so on—and Emmett's name did not come up. When are you going out there again?"

"I'm afraid to," Ella said, describing her vulnerability, clammy hands, and pounding heart. "The other night on the phone he told me he loved me. Last time I was out there he tried to kiss me. It would be too dangerous for me to go out there again."

"Did I ever tell you about the last time a male member of our species tried to kiss me?" Harriet asked.

"No," Ella said, surprised by the question. In the many years she had known Harriet, there had never been any discussion about Harriet's romantic life. Ella had just assumed there was none.

"I was fourteen," Harriet explained. "There was a party for the youth at the bishop's house. Some of us ended up in a back room, sitting on the floor in a circle, playing spin the bottle. The next thing I knew, the bottle was pointing at me, and a boy named Reed in a green scout shirt—covered with badges, medals, patches and beads—was crawling over to kiss me. I was so surprised and embarrassed that I tried to pull away as he pushed his lips against mine." Harriet paused, took a deep breath, then continued.

"His lips were wet, and oh so sweet, and had I known this would be the only time in my entire life a man—actually he was not a man, but a 12-year-old boy—would try to kiss me, I would have kissed him back, thrown my arms around him and not let go until the bishop pried us apart."

"I didn't know," Ella said, tears welling in her eyes over Harriet's touching monologue.

"Believe it or not, that was the biggest romantic thrill of my life," Harriet said, her eyes dry, her voice flat like the very life had been sucked out of her. "Everything else has been vicarious—books, movies, and even a little outrageous daydreaming.

"When I was a little girl," Harriet continued, "my father used to call me 'special.' That made me feel good. But you will never know what it is like to be fifty, fat and special at BYU. When someone holds a fireside for the special people, you want to die, after you go somewhere and throw up. You're told that if you are true and faithful you'll enjoy the opportunity of marriage in the next life—as a plural wife to someone like Bruce R. McConkie. Whoop-te-do.

"I have $33,000 in savings and retirement," Harriet continued. "I would pay every penny of it to change bodies with you for one week."

"Harriet, you are crazy," Ella said. "But if we could change bodies, what would you do?"

"I would go to the desert, find that Harvard cowboy, and have the time of my life. I would let him take me to Mt. Moriah. I would make love with him in the bunkhouse. I would come home and spend the rest of my life repenting, a smile on my face. And when people called me 'special,' it wouldn't bother me because I would know it to be true."

"Harriet, you are losing touch with reality," Ella cautioned.

"How can anyone who has never experienced reality be expected to be realistic?" Harriet asked as she started to cry.

"You think I should go out there again?" Ella asked.

"Life has passed me by," Harriet said. "Don't let it pass you by too."

"What about the commandments?"

"I'm not telling you to sin. If things work out, you can divorce George and marry the cowboy before you run off to the bunkhouse. People like you do that all the time."

Ella told Harriet how she had prayed for a sign to show her what to do, suggesting Harriet's words might be the sign she had been looking for.

"You probably never thought the Lord would give you such a big sign, big and special," Harriet said. "When are you going out to see Emmett again?"

"Next weekend," Ella said, finally making the decision to see Emmett again.

"Will you promise me one thing?" Harriet asked.

"Sure."

"Will you allow me to share what happens, vicariously?"

"Harriet, no matter what happens, you'll know every detail. It will be like we really did change places. You'll know

Chapter 11

everything. That's a promise."
   "Thank you."

Chapter 12

It was almost ten o'clock the next Friday night when Ella turned into the driveway at the ranch. Emmett's truck was by the house, and the lights were on, but when she knocked on the door he did not come to greet her. When she opened the door and called his name, he did not respond. She guessed he was out checking the last of the heifers that had not calved, so she started walking in that direction. A partial moon enabled her to see her way without any trouble.

Emmett was not at the heifer corral. Ella remembered he had a self-feeder in the bull pasture that occasionally needed checking to make sure the grain was getting down where the bulls could eat it. Emmett had been giving his bulls all the grain they would eat in preparation for the upcoming breeding season.

As she neared the bull pasture, Ella could see the 15 bulls milling around the feeder, and Emmett's silhouette in the foreground. Apparently the bulls had not been getting feed, and Emmett had just pushed it down to them, because all of the bulls were trying to eat at once—pushing and shoving, grunting and growling, in their efforts to find places at the feeder.

Ella decided to sneak up on Emmett. With the commotion of the bulls on the other side, she figured she could get close without him noticing.

She had approached within ten feet of Emmett when she realized all the noise was not coming from the bulls. Emmett was talking. There was no other person around, so she decided he must be talking to himself. Maybe he really was crazy. No. He was talking to the bulls. She stopped and listened.

"I'm not giving you guys all this $140-a-ton grain because you're handsome, or because I like you," Emmett was saying. "I'm doing it because you have a job to do, a job that requires strength and stamina.

"I've got 300 cows that need to be squirted full of semen in the next 60 days. And there's only 15 of you to do the job.

"Remember, this isn't an orgy, but a breeding program with order and rules. Here are the rules.

"One. The sentimental stuff humans associate with their breeding is strictly prohibited. I don't want any falling in love or fostering relationships. When you finish breeding one, move on to the next, then the next, and so on. Remember, faster is better. Time is money. The Bible says. 'Behold I come quickly.'

"Two. Discrimination is absolutely prohibited. Fat cows produce better calves than thin cows. And pretty cows don't produce any better calves than ugly cows. You can't see their faces anyway while you are breeding them.

"Three. No fighting. Unfortunately, the same hormones that make you breeding fools can also make you fighting fools. But this ranch isn't a bull ring or a rodeo arena. Anybody who would rather fight than breed will find a new career as a 4-H steer. Remember, there's only 15 of you and 300 of them, and many of the cows will need to be bred two

Chapter 12

or three times before they settle. There's plenty for
everybody. No need to fight over it.''

Ella remained silent, listening with fascination, wishing
she had brought paper and pencil so she could take notes.

"Those are the rules. Now for a word of caution,''
Emmett explained as the bulls continued to jostle each other
for positions at the feeder.

"After a few weeks of steady breeding, some of you
will get tired and lazy. Might get the idea you can bluff your
way through the season, jumping up and running around with
something hanging down every time you see my truck coming.
It won't work, because next fall, Doc Hunter will show up
with a box of rubber gloves. He'll reach into every cow and
tell me whether or not there's a calf in there. If very many
don't have calves, it's off to McDonald's with the lot of you.
I guess what I'm saying is you can't fake it. If you don't use
your Big Mac, you'll become one.''

As Emmett turned around to walk back to the house,
Ella started clapping.

"How long have you been here?'' he demanded.

"Long enough,'' she said. "When will you turn them
in with the cows?''

"Next week.''

"Let me ask you a question,'' she said.

"Go ahead.''

"Talking to your bulls like that—does it make you feel
jealous?''

"I don't understand.''

"You're turning them out to breed 300 cows, while you
don't even have one wife. Don't you feel left out?''

"Yes and no,'' he said thoughtfully. "There's an
emptiness in me, a yearning, that only a woman might satisfy.
But it has to be the right woman. But I have no need or desire
to be involved in an indiscriminate and wholesale breeding
program involving 300 females. The bulls can have that.
Should we go back now?''

"Maybe we should go up on the hill first,'' Ella

129

suggested as they started walking.

"I was thinking we could do it in the morning, when there's daylight."

"There might be enough moonlight, or do you have a flashlight? I am really curious. I'm afraid I won't sleep if I have to wait until morning."

"I'm afraid I won't sleep if we go now," Emmett said. "But if you want to do it by flashlight, there's one under the seat in my truck. But I'm warning you. Once you see what's up there you may want to get in your car and go back to Spanish Fork tonight."

"If I don't see what's on the hill I may get in my car and drive back to Spanish Fork anyway."

"Then I guess we do it," he said. They had reached his truck. Emmett picked up the flashlight and started towards the hill, where Ella followed him up a winding trail. In less than five minutes they reached the top. He still hadn't turned on the flashlight. But it was not difficult to see, thanks to a big slice of moon and thousands of stars giving light in a clear desert sky.

Ella looked around. She could see scattered clumps of sagebrush, an occasional boulder, and at the apex of the hill, a circle of rocks someone had piled up to form a crude shelter. She could see nothing unusual.

Emmett walked over to what Ella thought had been a boulder, and turned on his flashlight. It was not a big rock, but a headstone, and there was writing on it. She hurried to his side and looked closely at the stone. "Jennifer Hays" was the only writing on the smooth surface.

"You brought her body back here for burial?" Ella asked. Emmett nodded.

"Why didn't you want her in a cemetery?"

"It was her idea, not mine," Emmett explained. "One summer evening we came up here. We had been working hard, putting up a corral fence. She had been helping me. It was one of those perfect evenings, one I have never forgotten. Gray storm clouds were swirling over the top of the Deep

Chapter 12

Creek Mountains—growling, spitting out lightning, as storm clouds do that time of year. A cool breeze was moving down the valley from Blue Mass. Cows with new calves were grazing contentedly in the green meadows. Fish were rising on the Bunkhouse Pond. As I said, it was a perfect evening. We were standing close together, facing the valley, each with an arm around the other's waist.''

Emmett and Ella were standing side-by-side, facing the valley below. He took her hand. Their arms and shoulders were touching. She did not resist or pull away. He continued his story.

"Suddenly, Jennifer looks at me like she has a great idea and tells me she wants to be buried here. I say I'll do it, but that isn't good enough for her. She tells me I have to promise to bury her here. I'm thinking she won't die for sixty years, and that she'll die before me anyway, so it's an easy promise to make. How could I know she would die in a car wreck the next year?"

"So you brought her up here and buried her. I think that's beautiful."

"It's nice to have her close. I come up here often."

"I don't understand something."

"What?"

"Why did you think this would make me want to rush back to Spanish Fork?" Ella asked. "Why were you so upset when I almost came up here the day of the roping?"

"You haven't seen it all," Emmett said, placing his hand on Ella's waist to turn her to the west. He pointed his light on one of the other boulders, which turned out to be a headstone, too. "Mary Hays" was carved on the smooth surface.

"Your daughter?" Ella asked.

"My wife."

"You didn't tell me you were married twice."

"They both died in the same car wreck."

It didn't take more than a second for Ella to understand the full meaning of what Emmett was telling her. She pushed his hand from her waist, stepped back and turned to face him. There was anger in her voice when she spoke.

"You lied to me. You said you were not a polygamist."

"I'm not, at least not anymore."

"But you were. You should have told me."

"I was afraid you would leave."

"Your fears were well-founded."

Ella took a deep breath. She hadn't expected this. Her first thought was to get in the Jeep and drive back to Spanish Fork.

"It's scary to think I was considering divorcing poor George to marry a polygamist," she said, more to herself than to Emmett.

"I wish you would," he said.

"Sure," she responded, quickly and curtly. "A week after the honeymoon you would introduce me to Susan, who is going to be living in the bunkhouse. Or would you move me in the bunkhouse? Or would you keep us both in the house, in adjoining bedrooms, so you could run back and forth in the middle of the night, like your bulls do?"

"Stop it," Emmett said. "That part of my life is over. I will not be taking any more plural wives."

"But how could you be so dumb? I mean, you had it all. You were a returned missionary, a football hero ..."

"I was no hero."

"To George, everybody who starts, or even plays, is a hero. You went to Harvard. How could you turn your back on all that and become a polyg?"

"I don't like that slang word."

"I'm sorry. But how could you do it?"

"Do you really want to know? I mean, can you open your mind? You are operating from a narrower frame of reference than what you are capable of."

"I'm going home."

"No, please try to listen. To understand what I'm about to tell you, you have to transcend your Wasatch Front brand of 20th Century Republican Mormonism. People all over the

Chapter 12

world have their narrow little views of reality, their own unique sections of the big puzzle of life, formed by their own limited experience, combined with unique family, social and religious instruction. Because everyone thinks his or her view is the only correct one, there is a lot of conflict in the world. What makes it worse is most of us are not even aware that we have a unique view based on a narrow set of experiences.''

"OK, Mr. Philosopher, tell me how it happened. I'll honestly try to keep an open mind, but don't ask me to agree with you.'' Ella walked over to one of the boulders that was not a headstone and sat down, facing Emmett. He turned out the light.

"It happened in Boston, while I was in graduate school," he began. "Jennifer and I were newly married, and I think we were as happy as could be expected, considering the pressure associated with my studies. She worked and supported us, while I studied psychology.''

"That doesn't sound like an environment conducive to polygamous living,'' she added.

"But it was, in a roundabout way. I was in an environment of seeking and discovering truth. At dinner each night Jennifer and I would discuss what I was learning in the works of Pavlov, Skinner, Jung, Freud and others. I wasn't the only one learning. Both of us were involved.

"Our religious beliefs encouraged us in what we were doing. 'Know the truth, and the truth shall make you free.' From our religious training, we believed we were on a course of learning and discovery, challenge and struggle, that would eventually result in becoming like God. We realized we had a long way to go, but we were enjoying the journey.

"But it was different at church. I remember sitting in sacrament meeting one Sunday while a member of the stake high council was giving a speech. I looked around. Most of the men were asleep. Some of the women seemed to be listening while others tended restless babies. The children were writing notes, talking in whispers to each other, or just looking bored. Nobody was occupied in the eternal struggle to become like God.

"I remember thinking that as long as I was going to take time from my busy schedule to go to church, I might as well get something out of it. Mustering all my effort, I began listening to every word coming from that high councilman's mouth.

"It didn't take long to realize why no one was listening to him. Other than a few glib cliches, things I had known since I was ten years old, he had nothing to say. It was obvious he had spent little or no time preparing his talk, and was as anxious as everyone else to get the meeting over with so we could all go home and eat.

"The problem was that this meeting wasn't an isolated instance. Many, and perhaps most, seemed the same.

"About that time, on one of the first warm spring days, we went on a drive in the country. About noon we drove into a valley that was full of smoke—a forest fire."

"I've never heard of a forest fire in the spring," Ella said.

"It happens in the East where the leaves fall off the trees in the fall. If there's a few weeks of dry weather when the snow first melts in the spring, the leaves dry out and create a fire hazard. Anyway, we had driven right into the middle of a leaf-fed forest fire. As we continued to drive along, we could see no flames, but the smoke got thicker until we came to what appeared to be some kind of mobile firefighting headquarters. There were firetrucks, rows of tents and tables, and water cans with shoulder straps and squirt hoses.

"I got out of the car to see if they needed help. No one seemed to be in charge, and there was a lot of confusion. I strapped on one of the water cans, tested the wind, guessed where I thought most of the smoke was coming from, and headed up a rocky ridge, a natural fire barrier.

"Before I knew it, I was alone in a saddle, a break in the rock barrier I had been following. On my right, to the west, I could see the raging flames of the fire. A brisk west wind was blowing the fire in my direction. The saddle was only about 100 feet across, and to the east, my left, was a huge 10,000-acre valley that would be wasted once the fire got through the saddle. The rocky ridge would stop it everywhere else. There wasn't enough time to go for help, so I pumped up the pressure in my can and started spraying water on the fire. I would have succeeded if the wind had not been so strong.

"For a while I seemed to be holding the fire at bay, but the wind became stronger, the flames higher, and I was running out of water. Finally I put the can down, realizing I had lost the battle. Some of the things I had been reading in the scriptures about Enoch filled my heart. I stepped in front of the highest flames and raised my right arm to the square. In a loud voice, I commanded the wind, in the name of Jesus Christ and by the power of the Melchizedek Priesthood, to change directions. When I lowered my hand, the wind changed directions.

"I sat down on a rock, pondering what had happened. I began to cry. Some firefighters came along and told me I would have been fried if the wind had not changed directions. They put out the fire. It was easy with an east wind holding it back. I didn't say anything to them, but as I walked back to the car, I felt deeply moved by what had happened. Several times since, I have tried to control the wind, but without success.

"In the following months, Jennifer and I talked a lot about what had happened, and our religious beliefs in general. It seemed to us that while the church doctrines taught us we were on a course towards perfection, it didn't seem the church organization was pushing or pulling us in that direction. We went to meetings, did our home teaching and visiting teaching, paid fast offering and tithing, worried about this or that member who had had their feelings hurt, and that was about all. It was too easy, too boring, not enough challenge. If the people at church thought this was going to lead them to Godhood, we decided they had a big surprise coming. It was not going to happen. There had to be more.

"So we began to study, not the lesson manuals with the same old material we had learned in Primary, but the scriptures and other books, mainly historical in nature—the works of Joseph Smith, Brigham Young and John Taylor, and books about them. I remember calling friends in Provo to send me books I could not get in Boston. Keep in mind, this happened over a long period of time. I couldn't just drop my studies and dig into religion."

"What about Jennifer? How did she feel about all this?" Ella asked.

"We did it together. In fact, she had more time for this kind of reading than I did. She would find things and read them to me. We got into some of what today they call mysteries—consecration, calling and election, second endowments, united order, and polygamy.

"It was an intellectual pursuit. Our lives didn't change. I studied psychology during the week, and we went to church on Sundays."

"Did you feel like you were treading on dangerous ground?" Ella asked.

"No. We were seeking truth. How can there be anything wrong with that?"

"When or how did it change? I mean, how did you take the big step from an intellectual pursuit to actually taking a plural wife?"

"I can tell you exactly how it happened," Emmett said. "We were studying John Taylor's writings one Sunday afternoon when I made a startling discovery. Whenever John Taylor used terms like celestial marriage or the everlasting covenant of marriage, he was thinking plural marriage. To him, plural marriage and celestial marriage were synonymous terms, as they were with Brigham Young and Joseph Smith.

"With this new understanding, Jennifer and I opened the Doctrine and Covenants and began reading sections 131 and 132. It was as if the scriptures were reaching out of the book and grabbing us, telling us if we wanted a chance at

136

reaching the highest degree of the celestial kingdom we had better enter polygamy. If we didn't want to be damned, we had better become polygamists." He paused.

"Then what happened?" Ella asked, anxious for the story to continue.

"We quit studying. We stopped talking about it. It was like, after a long search of opening forbidden doors, we had suddenly discovered a monster, and now were afraid to face it. In private, I began praying for a sign, any kind of sign, showing me the way to go." He paused again.

"Did you get your sign?" Ella asked.

"Yes, but I'll tell you about that later. The next big event was coming home from classes one evening and finding Mary at the dinner table. Mary was a convert whom we had met at church. She was studying at one of the other schools in Boston. Frequently, we had friends over for dinner, so it did not seem strange having her there."

"Was she pretty?" Ella asked.

"Long black hair, olive complexion, trim figure. Yes, she was pretty."

"Without consulting you, Jennifer had picked a plural wife for you?" Ella asked.

"Yes. Right in the middle of dinner, Jennifer announced Mary was joining our family. I said I didn't know she was up for adoption. When they finished laughing, Jennifer made it clear that Mary was to become my plural wife."

"And you offered no objection, of course."

"For a few weeks there was a lot of talking, praying and fasting. But in the end, I consented. We all consented. I didn't think my inspiration was coming from the same place where my bulls get theirs. We found a justice of the peace, and with Jennifer as the witness, Mary and I were married. Since the apartment had two bedrooms, we decided to stay there until I finished school."

"Unbelievable," Ella said. "How in the world did you keep it secret?"

"We didn't. Within a few weeks there were rumors at church. When the stake president called me in, I gave him what I thought was a confidential confession. Afterwards he called my bishop, my former bishop, the general authorities, and so on. Pretty soon it seemed everyone knew."

"Did they hold a church court?" Ella asked.

"Yes. They told me it was a court of love, then proceeded to make me feel like an oversexed college student trying to drag innocent virgins down to hell. I felt awful. And I deserved what I got, but I didn't like them calling it a court of love. You are an English professor. Why does the Mormon Church have such a hard time with accurate usage of the English language?"

"So you were excommunicated?"

"All three of us. We felt so bad about it that we started talking about annulling the marriage with Mary. We had just about decided to do that when Mary tearfully announced she had missed her period. She was pregnant."

"So there was no turning back."

"I felt like Adam must have felt when he was cast out of the Garden of Eden, except I had two Eves instead of one. They told me in the court that with the excommunication, my spiritual growth would be stopped. I felt like the opposite happened. I no longer had a benevolent, well-organized church to guide me through life. I had to do it all myself, with the help of my wives. The struggle intensified, and I believe my spiritual growth accelerated as I fought the more difficult battle.

"I quit school. Took the rest of the money out of my education fund which my father left for me when he died, and moved out here."

"Why did you pick Pleasant Valley?"

"There are other fundamentalists in the area, people like us. Nobody had started a new church. We were just Mormons whom the Church had kicked out because we tried to live all the commandments. I didn't think my wives would feel like outcasts and misfits in Pleasant Valley. When our

138

Chapter 12

children started going to school, there would be other children like them. So I put a down payment on the ranch, bought a few cows, and started my new life as a polygamist in the desert.''

"Then the car wreck. Thank you, Emmett Hays, for telling me your story," Ella said, standing up, trying to figure out if she wanted to go home or stay.

"I'm not finished," he said.

"Don't you dare show me another headstone," she said.

"There is one more," he said, pointing the flashlight in a different direction. She stepped forward to read the inscription. Rebecca Hays.

"You had three wives?"

"No. Rebecca was my little girl, Mary's daughter. She died in the wreck with her mother." Emmett paused, turned out the light, and walked over to Ella.

"I want to be buried here, too," he said. "That'll be my last wish when I die."

"We almost forgot something," Ella said, changing the subject. "You said you would tell me later about the sign you were praying for."

"The sign came too late," Emmett explained. "It was the car wreck which killed the three people I loved most in the world." His voice was breaking. Even in the semi-darkness she could see tears in his eyes. "Had I not gone into polygamy they would still be alive. I should have followed the leaders of the Church instead of what I found in the history and scriptures."

"You're saying polygamy is wrong?"

"No. I am saying it was wrong for me. I was too lazy. And my laziness killed Jennifer and Mary."

"You're talking like a child now," Ella objected. "You can't blame yourself for an automobile accident. You weren't even there."

"It was my fault. Do you remember when I was telling you about the odometer on my old Suburban, the one that

139

quick working?"

"Vaguely."

"I didn't fix it, and a year later it just started working again."

"Yes. I remember. You said it was the most false lesson you had ever learned."

"The truck that killed Jennifer and Mary had a steering problem," he explained. "It was a 1980 Ford 3/4 ton four-wheel-drive pickup. Sometimes when the steering fluid would get low, the steering wheel would turn real easy like it wasn't connected to the front wheels. The wheels would not turn with it. I'd add some steering fluid, then it would work just fine.

"The steering column had been damaged and was coming apart. There wasn't enough strength in the column to turn the front wheels without the power assist motor, which had a leak and kept needing more fluid."

"This is getting too technical for me," Ella said.

"The point is that I am no mechanic," Emmett confessed. "I hate working on cars, trucks and farm machinery. Some people like that kind of thing. I don't, so I get other people to do it when I can. I hate greasing bearings, replacing brake shoes, or even changing oil, so I avoid those kinds of tasks."

"You, and most other people."

"Other people don't ignore steering failures, especially on vehicles driven by loved ones," he argued. "They were headed into Provo, had just crossed Sand Pass. Jennifer was driving too fast, probably about 70. Suddenly the steering wheel was spinning free, while the truck was veering towards the shoulder. She hit the brakes, but it was too late. The truck went off the road and rolled 14 times. Had Jennifer not lived long enough to tell about it, I would never have known for sure that faulty steering was the cause of the accident. My laziness was the cause of the accident. They are dead because I was too lazy to fix the steering. My laziness killed Jennifer and Mary, and little Rebecca. God gave me my sign. Now I spend my time with cows and ropers, no longer worthy to be with people I love—at least that's the way I felt until you came along.

"You see, original sin really does exist. It is the laziness in all of us. Some have it more than others, but all have it. It is the force of entropy, the power of the devil, that is pulling us all down, holding us back from the godly potential we all possess. It destroyed my family.

"Evil people hate light because it shows them for what they really are. They hate goodness because it shows their badness. They hate love because it exposes their laziness, which is evil carried to its ultimate extreme. Ultimately there is only one enemy, and his name is laziness."

"You said the three of you, in Boston, fasted and prayed about the decision to enter polygamy," Ella said. "You said your prayers were answered."

"Yes, I said that," he responded. "I truly believe the spirit of God is there to guide us, all of us. When we make bad choices, it is usually because we are too lazy to hang in there until we know what God really wants. In my case, after that first dinner, I wanted Mary. She was one of the most beautiful creations God ever placed on this earth. I wasn't about to talk her and Jennifer out of what they wanted to do. Ella, you are listening to a damned man."

"In some ways I feel I am listening to a great man," she said. "Life's tragedies make some people bitter or afraid. They have made you wise."

"If greatness has anything to do with the capacity to suffer, then I am a great man," Emmett said. He took Ella by the hand and they started down the little trail leading to the bunkhouse.

She told him about the proposed article on the Moriah wilderness.

"Will you take me?" she asked.

"As I said on the hill, maybe it's time for me to pursue relationships beyond those with cattle and ropers. I'll take you in the morning."

They reached the bunkhouse. Before entering, Ella

turned to face Emmett. She kissed him on one cheek, then the other. His only response was a warm "Thank you."

Chapter 13

The next morning, Ella was awakened by the sound of a truck entering the yard. It was barely light, and the sun had not yet come up. She thought it strange that someone would drop by so early. She hoped something wasn't wrong. Ella crawled out of bed and looked out the window. She recognized the man who got out of the truck and hurried to the front door of the house. It was Wade Hanks.

Ella watched as Emmett opened the door and listened to what Wade had to say. She could tell by the expressions on both men's faces that the news wasn't good. She couldn't hear anything Wade was saying, and since she wasn't dressed, she made no effort to join the two men. A minute later, Wade hurried back to his truck, got in, and roared out of the yard. Emmett disappeared inside the house.

Ella showered and dressed as quickly as possible, hoping the news wasn't something that would prevent them from going to Moriah. As soon as she was ready, she hurried to the house.

When she saw Emmett's face, she knew something

terrible had happened.

"What is it?" she asked.

"Billy Thunder. Killed late last night."

"How did it happen?" she asked.

"Ran into a power pole, somewhere over by Wendover. The authorities said he was going over 90 miles per hour. He was drunk. It will be a closed casket funeral."

"I'm so sorry," Ella said, feeling genuine remorse. Impulsively she stepped forward and put her hand on Emmett's shoulder.

"I'm sorry, too," he said. "Billy was a good friend. Came over three or four times a week while he was learning to rope. Things won't be the same. Have to get a new roping partner."

"Should we cancel the trip to Moriah?" she asked, stepping back, removing her hand from his shoulder.

"Funeral's not until Tuesday. Won't get anything done around here today, not now. Might as well go to Moriah, if you don't mind going with someone who has just lost a good friend. I may not be very good company."

An hour later they were driving down the Pleasant Valley road. They were in Emmett's truck, pulling a four-horse trailer. Geronimo, Tithing, and Emmett's pack mule, Martha, were in the trailer. Emmett had reminded Ella that the best photos would be available only when the sun was low in the sky, evening and morning. To get these kinds of photos they would have to stay overnight on the mountain. The pack outfit for the mule included sleeping bags, foam pads, a tent, picket ropes for the horses, cooking gear and food.

"I wonder why it is," Emmett said, "when you get some bad news, like this morning, you feel like something has been sucked out of you, like you are ten years older."

"I suppose aging is an emotional process, as well as a physical one," Ella responded, but not liking the depressing nature of the conversation, she decided to lighten things up.

"Do you know how a woman can tell when she's getting old?" she asked.

Chapter 13

"How?"

"When she goes to the chiropractor for a routine tune-up and he doesn't make her take her clothes off."

"It's not so simple with men," Emmett shot back, smiling for the first time that day. "First you forget names, then faces. Next, you forget to zip your pants up. But the final insult, the last step into irreversible senility, I've been told, is when you forget to zip your pants down."

By now, both of them were laughing. It was a beautiful May morning, with a bright sun in a deep blue desert sky. Both of them were wearing dark glasses. It would get warmer on the desert floor, but temperatures would be comfortable on the mountain where Emmett and Ella were going.

As they drove out of the valley bottom onto the bench, they could see the snow-capped peaks of Moriah to the south, with the table in the foreground. Ella felt her heart quicken, like she was embarking on a great adventure. And she couldn't think of anyone she would rather share it with than Emmett Hays.

Emmett explained there were three trails leading to the table from the east side of the mountain. The Smith Canyon trail was the closest, and normally the one he used, but this time he wanted to use the Hendry's Canyon trail, the one farthest to the south. He said the horseback ride was a little longer that way, but it was worth it. He said the trail wound beneath some spectacular rock formations, through some ancient stands of quakies, and along a small stream full of fish, at least at the higher elevations. The trail led through some of the oldest stands of bristlecone pines just before reaching the table. This is where the best campsites were located, especially in late summer and fall when water was scarce, because there was a good spring just below the trail as it reached the table.

"Now that I know everything about you," Ella began as they turned south on the main road leading to Moriah, "tell me why you named my horse Tithing."

"When I was excommunicated they told me I couldn't

pay tithing,'' he explained. ''So when I moved out here I took some of the money I had been saving for tithing and bought me a horse. It was a yearling filly, and since she didn't have a name yet, it seemed appropriate to name her Tithing.''

''Do you think you'll ever pay tithing to the Church again?'' Ella asked.

''A while back I was riding my horse through the sagebrush sand hills behind the church at Trout Creek. It was Sunday morning, and I was looking for some stray cows. It was one of the first warm spring days, so they had opened all the windows and doors at the church. I could hear the congregation singing an opening song. It made me feel like I wanted to go inside, like that's where I belonged. I got off my horse and tied him to a tree. I stretched out on the warm sand on an east-facing slope where I could best hear the sounds coming from the building. A little while later I heard the sacrament song. It felt like someone was rubbing a soothing salve on my wounded heart. I fell asleep, and was awakened later by the closing song.''

''Sleeping, just like the men inside the church,'' Ella teased.

''I had never paid much attention to the songs when I was active in the Church,'' he said. ''When you go ten years without hearing them, you think you have forgotten, but you haven't. When you hear them again you feel all choked up, and want to be part of all that again. The next time I was in town I bought some Mormon Tabernacle Choir tapes.''

''So you see yourself getting back in the Church?'' she asked.

''I hope so,'' Emmett responded. ''I feel like I am being guided in that direction. I don't think it's an accident that you came into my life when you did.''

''I'm no missionary,'' she said.

''Then what are you?''

''A woman who has it all—a temple marriage, a family, a successful career—but who feels like something is lacking.''

''They call that feeling the mid-life crisis,'' he

explained. "Mine was activated ten years early because of an automobile accident. But one act can fix both of our mid-life crises."

"And what is that?" she asked.

"Divorce George and marry me."

"All of my life I have been taught that divorce is wrong."

"I think it could more accurately be described as hard," Emmett argued. "What's bad is spending your life in a mismatched, incompatible marriage. You get into it when you're 20 and your good judgment is being clouded by overflowing hormones, and spend the rest of your life gutting it out."

"I know a lot of people who are doing just that," Ella responded.

"Why do they stay?"

"Probably because they think it's the right thing to do, that they'll get their reward in heaven."

"That's what they tell you if you ask," he argued, "but the real reasons are very different."

"OK, Mr. Philosopher, tell me the real reasons people in mismatched marriages don't get divorced."

"Lack of money, lack of courage, and laziness are the three big ones," he said. "The people in abusive marriages have to get out to survive. The rest start thinking about how much money it will cost—not just for the lawyers, but the additional housing, transportation, insurance, and things like that incurred after the divorce. Afraid of criticism from peers and family, upsetting the children, and so on, it's just a lot easier, requires less money and less courage, to leave things the way they are and hope for better things in the next world."

"I feel a little hypocritical wondering what happened to the old fashioned concept that marriage vows are sacred and binding," Ella said, "not to be discarded at the first sign of incompatibility. 'For better or for worse,' seems to be a forgotten phrase. Nobody said marriage is supposed to be easy. I hope that if I marry you, you won't run off to see the lawyer the first time we have a disagreement."

"How about the second time?" he teased.

"How about the hundredth time?" she added. "Seriously, I don't know if I have what it takes to divorce George?"

"Both of you have good jobs, so the money shouldn't be a serious problem," Emmett said. "The fact that you earned a Ph.D. and are running around the west desert gathering information for articles you don't have to do tells me you are not lazy. I don't know about the courage. Can you tell George you are leaving him? Can you tell your children you are kicking their father out of the house? Can you tell your department chairman that he is going to have a divorcee on his staff at a school where, more than any other college in the country, divorce is looked down upon?

"It's much easier to just stay where you are," Emmett continued. "That's what most people do. You see, contrary to what churches say, divorce is not the easy way out in most marriages. The easiest thing to do is to stay. In your case, all you have to do is buy some earplugs to shut out Paul James and Jay Monson, and say goodby to Emmett Hays. The other alternative will require much more effort and courage."

"You've convinced me," Ella teased. "Turn around and take me back to the ranch. I'm going home to George."

"The only way you can go back to your car now is to jump out of a moving vehicle and hike across 15 miles of uninhabited desert. I'm not stopping, nor am I turning back."

"Stop the truck. I have to go to the bathroom," she laughed.

"I'm not stopping because I think you are lying," Emmett said. "In case you're not, use this." He handed her an empty peanut can.

"You're kidnapping me," she said.

"I guess you can call it that, if you want to."

"Are you going to rape me, too?"

"Is that what you would like?" he asked, holding up

148

Chapter 13

his arm when she threw the peanut can at him.

"Stop the truck," she demanded.

"There is only one thing you can say that will get me to stop the truck and turn around."

"Tell me what it is so I can say it."

"First, you must promise to be totally honest, not to lie."

"I promise."

"Are you afraid to go with me to Moriah? Are you worried, even a little, that I might hurt you, rape you, or abuse you in any way? Tell me the truth. If you are frightened, even a little, I will take you back."

Ella thought about the nights she had spent in the bunkhouse, with or without the door locked. It didn't matter. Emmett had a key. Many times she had looked deep into his face, into his eyes. Never had she felt anything to make her afraid or want to flee. And she did not feel that way now.

"I am not afraid," she admitted. "Not even a little."

"Good," he said, as he pushed down on the gas pedal for more speed.

There wasn't a lot of room to maneuver the truck and trailer at the Moriah trailhead, but Emmett turned the truck around and pointed it downhill before turning off the engine and unloading the horses.

It didn't take long to get on the trail. Emmett had saddled the horses back at the ranch, and the sawbuck was already on the mule. After tightening the cinches Emmett found a handscale in the front of the horse trailer. It had a handle on one end, and a hook on the other. He used it to weigh the two canvas panniers that contained their camp outfit. When he was finished, he moved several items from one pannier to the other, then weighed them again.

"Why are you doing that?" Ella asked. "They can't be very heavy."

"Forty-two pounds each," he said. "But the weight is not important, only that they weigh the same, so Martha will be carrying a balanced load."

"And if the load is not balanced?"

"Martha will be uncomfortable, will get sores on her back, and will tire faster."

Emmett secured a pannier to each side of the sawbuck, then threw on the top pack containing the sleeping bags and foam pads. The mule was ready.

Each saddle horse carried saddlebags and a canteen. The jackets were tied behind the saddles. Ella's camera bag was attached to her saddle horn where it would be easy to get at.

As she mounted her horse, Ella noticed Emmett was wearing a gun belt. "Why are you bringing a gun?" she asked.

"I'm taking a beautiful woman into a remote wilderness," he said. "I want to be able to protect her."

"From what? Bears?"

"Everybody thinks the big cities are the most dangerous places, and they probably are, but when the criminal types get into the back country they have a tendency to feel they are outside the reach of the law and can do what they want. A rapist who would leave you alone in New York City because he didn't want to risk arrest wouldn't hesitate to come after you out here. Fortunately there are not many people like that here, hopefully none. But I carry a gun just in case.

"If the mule runs off with our food I can use my gun to get us a grouse for supper," he continued. "If a horse breaks a leg, my gun allows me to put him out of his misery, quickly and painlessly. With a gun at my side I sleep better at night." They started up the trail, Emmett leading the way.

To Ella's surprise, Emmett was not leading the mule. He had secured Martha's lead rope to the front of her sawbuck, leaving her free to go where she wished, even to graze.

"Won't the mule run off?" Ella asked.

"Won't leave the horses, especially the mare you're riding," Emmett explained. "Mules fall in love with mares, and don't want to be left behind. Don't worry about Martha. She'll be our shadow all day."

Chapter 13

And so it was. Martha was never more than 50 feet from the horses. Sometimes she would fall behind, nibbling on grass or bull clover, but as soon as she noticed the horses were leaving her behind, she would gallop to catch up.

Ella was enjoying herself, feeling the confident gait of the horse beneath her, taking in the breathtaking scenery, keeping an eye on Emmett's broad shoulders. She was glad she had not talked him into taking her back to the ranch.

After a little over an hour of riding, they stopped for a break under a large cottonwood tree. Sitting in the shade by the stream, they shared a sandwich, several cookies, and sips of water from the same canteen.

"I wonder if the Goshutes bury possessions with the dead," Emmett said. "I know the Utes do it, believing the spirit of the deceased can take possessions with them to the world of spirits."

"You mean things like bows and arrows, guns, knives, things like that?" she asked.

"Living things too, like horses, dogs, even wives. But they don't do that any more. I know a man in Fort Duschesne who said they killed 300 horses when his grandfather died. The smell was so bad nobody could go near the grave for years. When I get home I'm going to call Billy's mother and ask if the Goshutes have the same custom. If they do, I'm going to give her a new rope to bury with Billy—a brand-new Rocky Mountain brand, medium hard. That was his favorite rope for catching heels."

"That first day we met," Ella said, changing the subject, "when I hit the deer, how did you know I was from Spanish Fork?"

"I don't know. It just came out, without thinking, while I was talking. It was the same thing when I said something about you having two children."

"It can't be a coincidence, not when two things like that happen in a row," she said.

"I remember when I was at Harvard, sitting in the classroom," he explained. "When the professor would explain

151

a new idea, I didn't feel like I was learning something, but like I was remembering something, and the professor's words were merely digging the truth out of me, dragging it from somewhere deep inside so I could recognize it like an old friend and place it on the front shelf in my conscious mind. Have you ever felt that way when you were learning something new?"

"I think so. Yes."

"It's as if we are born with a micro chip in our genes containing all knowledge and all wisdom. As we learn and grow we bring bits and pieces of it into our conscious minds where we can use them. Learning is discovering things that have been within us all along."

"It's too bad you didn't finish school," Ella said. "It is too bad you are spending your life being a nursemaid to cows, and roping steers. Has it ever occurred to you that you ought to be doing more?"

"All the time," Emmett said, getting up. "Maybe ten years of mourning for Jennifer and Mary is long enough."

"I think they would want you to move ahead," Ella offered.

"They say the people in the best marriages are engaged in mutual psychotherapy," he observed. "I want to thank you for the nudge, even though you are not my wife." They got on their horses and resumed their journey up the trail to Moriah.

As the day progressed, the wind began to blow, not so much in the canyon where they were following the trail, but on the ridgetops. Gray clouds began to appear in the sky.

They rode by the ancient remains of a cabin and some corrals. Emmett could only speculate who might have lived there. Perhaps a herder, a miner, maybe even outlaws hiding from the law. Beyond the cabin, the quakies were the thickest and tallest Ella had ever seen.

"Good country for trees," Emmett said. "Some of the biggest firs you'll ever see farther up. And the bristlecones are 3,000 years old. Maybe the people who built the cabin thought they would live 200 years. But I guess they didn't.''

When they reached the spring where the little creek originated, they had to put on their jackets and gloves. The wind was blowing harder, and the sky was nearly covered with a fast-moving cloud cover.

"The picture-taking will probably have to wait until morning," Emmett said, as they left the canyon bottom onto some switchbacks leading to the table. Even in the cold wind, the horses were sweating as they toiled up the mountain trail. Emmett stopped occasionally to allow the animals to catch their wind.

When the trail reached the top of the ridge, Ella saw the first bristlecone pines. They were similar in appearance to pinion pine, but larger, with more curves and twists in the trunks and major branches. She thought this might be a function of living on a windy mountaintop. It was too early in the season for her to see the little blue pinecones Emmett had told her about.

When Emmett finally stopped, in a thick stand of pine trees just below the table, it was beginning to rain. The sky was black with clouds, and the wind showed no sign of letting up. Five or six deer, all bucks, bounded to the top of a rocky ridge and disappeared from view onto the Moriah table, which Emmett said extended for three miles beyond the ridge.

Emmett dismounted, tied up his horse and the mule, loosened their cinches, and began removing the top pack and panniers. Ella tied her horse to a tree, loosened the cinch and removed her camera bag from the saddle horn. The rain had stopped. She told Emmett she wanted to hike to the top of the ridge so she could see the table and maybe get a few pictures before dark. She knew she wouldn't get any good scenery shots, but perhaps she would get lucky and catch a bighorn sheep or herd of deer running from the storm to find shelter.

"I can't go with you," he said. "I have to set up camp and take care of the horses. You are not familiar with the landmarks on the table. You could get lost, especially in a storm.''

"I won't go far," Ella promised as she buttoned up the top button on her jacket.

"See that lone tree on top of the ridge?" Emmett said, pointing to a distant tree. "Don't let it out of your sight. Once you get back to the tree, it's downhill to camp."

"OK," she promised, turning and heading up the hill. It felt good to be on the ground again, walking instead of riding. In the cold wind the walking made her warm. Frequently she had to stop and catch her breath. The cold air was thin. Emmett said their camp was just below the 10,000 foot level.

When Ella reached the tree, the view was disappointing. All she could see was relatively flat, rocky ground disappearing into clouds and fog. After taking a good look at the tree, and the camp below where Emmett was fighting the wind to put the tent up, Ella ventured forward onto the table. Occasionally, she looked back at the tree, knowing she could not get lost as long as she could see it.

Suddenly, ahead of her in the fog, she saw a gray form. At first Ella thought it might be a bush or a big rock. But then it seemed to move. She continued to walk towards it, slowly and quietly. It moved again, probably a deer, or a bighorn sheep. Maybe a mountain lion. Ella's heart was pounding. The wind was blowing in her face, carrying her sounds and smells away from the thing she was looking at, giving her hope that in the cover of the fog she might get close enough for a photo. She continued her stalk, one step at a time, slowly, carefully.

She pulled her camera out of the bag and removed the lens cover. Quickly, she checked the shutter speed and made sure the automatic f-stop was working. Then she pushed the camera under the bottom of her jacket so water wouldn't get on the lens, and continued to move forward.

As she drew closer, the gray form began to take a more precise shape. It had legs, and a head. It was grazing.

When the head came up to look around, Ella stopped. When the gray head went back to the ground, she stepped

154

closer, her hands ready to bring the camera out from under her jacket at the right moment.

Gradually she realized she was stalking a deer. As she got closer she could see it was a buck because it had antlers. But there was something strange about the antlers. They were thicker than any she had seen, and instead of growing up, they were growing straight out.

She stopped, pulled the camera out from under her jacket, and took several pictures while the buck continued to graze. The sounds of film winding and the shutter clicking were carried away by the wind. The deer continued to graze.

After four pictures, Ella decided to move to her right, hoping to get some photos from a different angle. She kept her eyes on the deer as she moved.

Suddenly her foot slipped, probably on a wet rock. When she attempted to replant the foot on solid ground, it slipped again. She lost her balance and found herself rolling down a hill into a gully. Her first thought was to wonder if she had frightened the deer. She was able to stop rolling and get to her feet in time to watch the deer disappear into the fog.

Ella checked her camera. It was wet, but didn't appear to be damaged. She wiped off as much moisture as possible and returned it to the camera bag. The rain began to fall again. It was getting dark. Ella's trousers and jacket were soaked, and she was beginning to shiver. She wished she were back at camp, standing by a blazing campfire, talking to Emmett.

She looked around and could not see her landmark, the tree. She was not alarmed, because she had rolled into a gully. She climbed to the nearest high point, and looked again. On seeing the tree, she felt more than a little relieved. Before starting towards it, she looked around again, hoping that from the top of the hill she might get another glimpse of the deer.

Instead of seeing the deer, she saw another tree. It looked more like the landmark than the first one. The two trees were in opposite directions and she wasn't sure which one to walk towards. The rain was beginning to turn to snow. In ten minutes it would be dark, and with the thick cloud cover there would be no light from the stars and moon.

She was forced to gamble, and she realized her gamble was a desperate one. She was soaked, and her teeth were chattering from the cold. If Ella picked the wrong tree, by the time she found out she would not be able to see the other one. She didn't have a flashlight or matches. And even if she did, she wouldn't be able to build a fire because everything around her was wet.

The table was three miles across. She could wander all night without finding camp. And what about the thousand-foot cliffs Emmett had described on the northeast side of the table. She had no idea which way was northeast.

In the howling wind, Emmett would not hear her cries for help. He would come looking for her, but in the fog and clouds, he would not be able to see the familiar landmarks, and he would become lost in the night too. What if he found her, and they remained lost together. They would die in each other's arms. At least that would be better than dying alone. Ella hurried towards the tree, praying it was the right one.

It was not. When she reached the tree, there was no steep dropoff on the other side, no camp below. She looked back in the general direction where she had seen the other tree, but she had come too far, and it was too dark. Ella sat down under the tree, telling herself this was no time to panic.

She guessed she had not come more than half a mile from the landmark tree, and it was no more than half a mile from camp. If she wandered around in the darkness, the chances were fifty-fifty that she would wander farther from camp. Maybe she would hurt herself in the dark, or wander off one of the cliffs. If she stayed where she was, under the tree, hoping Emmett would find her, he would have to do it quickly, or Ella would die of hypothermia. How long could she stay alive, cold and wet, with the wind continuing to howl? She noticed that all the rain had turned to snow, and guessed that in two or three hours she would be dead.

Should she crawl under the tree and hope Emmett would find her before she died of hypothermia, or should she wander into the night and risk becoming hopelessly lost? Ella guessed her chances of walking in a straight line to camp were nearly impossible.

She asked herself what Emmett would do in her shoes. Then she thought of a better question. What would Emmett do in Emmett's shoes? When she didn't come back, he would come looking for her. Because it was almost dark he would bring a flashlight. He would go to the top of the hill to the landmark tree. Since he had told Ella to keep that tree in view, that's exactly where he would go. When he didn't see her, he would call for her, then he would carefully move forward onto the table, not wanting to lose his own bearings. If she stayed at the tree he would be close to her. Maybe Ella would hear his voice, maybe he would hear her cries for help. The big question was time. How long could she remain conscious, staying at the tree, doing nothing?

Then Ella realized she didn't have to lay down and die. Working muscles generated heat. If she couldn't enjoy the heat of a fire, she would make her own heat. She would hike in a circle around the tree. She could hike around the tree all night, if necessary. She had been concerned about a growing bulge around her hips. Tonight she would burn it off, all of it. In her article Ella would call her experience the Moriah hypothermia diet—guaranteed to take off ten pounds of ugly fat in one night. She jumped to her feet and started jogging around the tree. It was dark now. When her body began to feel warmer, she slowed to a brisk walk. After every revolution Ella stopped, raised her hands to her mouth and called to Emmett. She listened briefly for a response, and then began her next revolution around the tree.

Ella counted the revolutions, guessing that would help keep her mind focused on the business at hand, hiking around the tree. Counting the steps, counting the revolutions, shouting as loud as she could every time she stopped. She knew she had to do this all night, or die. Her toes and fingers were already numb, but let them freeze, she would keep going forever if necessary. Ella put her head down and marched.

After the eighty-third revolution around the tree, Ella thought she heard a crack, like a tree limb breaking. Strange, she thought. She hadn't noticed any trees big enough to make that loud of a cracking sound. Then she realized the wind was blowing less than before. Limbs wouldn't be cracking now. The snowing had mostly stopped, but the snow on the ground was not melting.

What had made that cracking sound? Emmett's gun, of course. Why had she not thought of that sooner? She stopped, trying to calculate the direction from which the sound of the gunfire had come. She called to Emmett. No response.

Crack. She heard it again. In total blackness, Ella started towards the sound, believing that if Emmett fired twice, he would fire again. Every twenty steps she called his name.

Crack. She heard the third shot and adjusted her course, heading more to the left. After the fifth shot, she saw a pinpoint of flickering light. Emmett's flashlight. A few seconds later she heard him calling her name. She called back.

She ran the last twenty yards, throwing herself into his arms, kissing his icy cheeks, kissing his eyes, his mouth, trying to squeeze the very breath out of him. Emmett had saved her from the very jaws of death—if he knew the way back to camp.

"Do you know the way back?" she asked.

"If the wind hasn't changed. Earlier it was coming from the northwest. I came looking for you with it blowing against the front left side of my face. It'll blow against the back of my right ear as we go back to camp. If the wind hasn't changed, we'll be in camp in ten minutes." He pointed the flashlight in front of them so they wouldn't stumble on rocks.

Ella grabbed Emmett's hand as they started back to

Chapter 13

camp, squeezing tightly with her numb fingers, never wanting to let go.

Chapter 14

Emmett was upset with himself for not bringing a tent stove or lantern. On winter hunting trips he usually brought such items along, but not in May when one expected more mild weather.

Ella couldn't seem to stop shivering for very long, no matter how close she stood to the blazing campfire. Her clothing was wet. Whichever side was away from the fire soon became cold in the freezing wind. Even with Emmett handing her cups of steaming hot chocolate, she had difficulty suppressing the chattering teeth.

"We've got to get you out of those wet clothes," he said.

"I brought an extra polyester shirt," she said, "but thinking we wouldn't be up here very long, I didn't bring anything else."

"Did you bring any pajamas?" he asked.

"No, I was planning on sleeping in my clothes."

Emmett rummaged through one of the panniers and

found a red and black wool shirt and a pair of heavy socks. He told her to go in the tent, get out of the wet clothing, slip on the wool shirt and socks, and crawl into one of the sleeping bags, where she could keep warm until he was able to dry her clothes.

Ella took the rapidly fading flashlight with her into the tent and zipped the flap shut. The inside of the tent wasn't any warmer than outside. The only difference was that the wind wasn't blowing. Ella's hands were shaking, and she felt so weak. She was surprised how much effort it took to remove her soaked boots and socks. She found it so difficult to remove her wet jeans, which seemed frozen to her skin, that she wanted to call to Emmett to help. But she didn't. She pushed, wiggled and pulled until she finally got them off. She could never remember feeling so exhausted in her entire life. All she wanted to do was lie back and go to sleep. But she couldn't.

Taking her wet shirt and bra off required so much effort Ella felt sick to her stomach. Biting hard on her lower lip, she removed the rest of her clothing and slipped into the wool shirt, the first warm thing she had felt since leaving the fire. She tried to do up the buttons, but her hands were shaking too much. She did manage, however, to get the big socks on, before crawling into a bulky blue sleeping bag.

Another big disappointment. Ella had expected the sleeping bag to feel warm, but it was like crawling into a bag of ice. She hoped all the chattering wasn't chipping her teeth.

A minute later Emmett came into the tent. He said the wind was blowing harder than ever, but the weather was getting a little warmer. The snow seemed to be turning back to rain. He said the coffee pot with the hot chocolate water had blown over, and with the flashlight batteries almost dead he didn't think in the dark he could find the spring to get more water. He was having trouble keeping the fire going, between the rain, blowing wind, and the fact that he had built it on flat ground in accordance to wilderness restrictions against fire circles and pits. The wind was blowing the coals out from under the wood.

Rather than fight the storm any longer, Emmett had decided to come to bed. The dying flames of the fire cast a little light on the tent wall as he pulled off his wet boots and jeans and slipped into his sleeping bag. By the time he had pulled the zipper up to his chin, the last of the flames had died, and it was totally dark.

"Good night," he said cheerfully.

"Emmett, I'm afraid," Ella said.

"Things could be a lot worse, you know. We have warm sleeping bags, and a tent to protect us from the storm."

"My sleeping bag isn't warm," she said, her voice weak. "It felt like a bag of ice when I crawled in, and it still feels that way. There is no feeling in my feet and hands."

"But your teeth are no longer chattering," he said reassuringly.

"That's what frightens me. It's like my body is giving up. I'm too cold to shiver. My systems are shutting down. I'm fighting to stay awake. If I go to sleep, I don't think I will wake up, at least not on this side of the veil."

Emmett sat up. He reached in her sleeping bag and felt her hand, then the bare skin on her back.

"It appears we have a severe case of hypothermia," he said, trying to sound analytical and scientific, but there was a distinct sense of alarm in his voice.

"I read once where the best thing to do in a case like this is to throw the subject into a bath of hot water," he explained nervously. "If I had only called the weather service, or brought along a tent heater. My damn laziness killed my wives, and now I've got you ..."

"Emmett," Ella said sharply. "Don't give me another lecture on laziness. I'm in trouble. Do something. Anything. Please."

"There's only one thing to do," he said, crawling out of his sleeping bag. "Whether you like it or not, I'm getting in your sleeping bag with you. Roll over."

Before she could think about what he had said, or offer

a response, Emmett was inside Ella's sleeping bag, his chest against her back, his strong arms around her, pulling her close.

"If someone was holding a contest tonight to determine the most frigid woman in the world, I think you would win," he teased. Ella was too weak and scared to respond.

His breathing felt deliciously warm against the back of her head and neck. She began to shiver, her body systems deciding to help in the warming process. Emmett's warmth, like electricity, flowed from him to her, warming her body first, then her legs and arms, and finally her feet and hands. After awhile the shivering stopped, and the sleeping bag felt warm. The only thing that prevented Ella from falling into an exhausted and comfortable sleep was the sharp pain in her fingers and toes as the feeling returned. But in a while that went away, too.

Ella decided that having Emmett in her bag was better than a hot bath. In fact, the sleeping bag was getting hot, and it felt wonderful.

That's when Emmett began to pull the zipper down so he could get out.

"What are you doing?" she demanded.

"I think the hypothermia is under control," he said. "Your bag should stay warm now, so I'm going back to mine."

"Please don't."

"I have to. My driving force to help a damsel in distress is being replaced by another driving force. I have to go."

"No, you don't," Ella said, rolling over in Emmett's arms, wrapping her leg around his, kissing him on the mouth. He kissed her back. Neither seemed to notice or care that the zipper was down.

Chapter 15

When Ella awakened, glorious sunshine was bursting through the open tent flap. Emmett was gone. Her clothes were hanging on a line by the blazing fire.

The horses and mule, with long picket ropes tied to their front feet, were eagerly grazing the wet grass. The rain had washed away the snow, except where it had drifted next to bushes and rocks.

Beyond the horses the sun had just come up over the House Mountains. Ella could see other mountains whose names she did not know. The valleys below the peaks were oceans of blue-gray haze, still waiting for the morning sun to bring them light and warmth.

Beyond the horses the bristlecone pines glistened, washed clean by the night storm, ready to have their pictures taken. Pictures. That's why she was here. The best morning light would soon be gone. There was no time to lose. Ella left on the wool shirt Emmett had given her, pulled on her jeans which were still damp, found some dry stockings in her saddlebags and put them on, then slipped into her wet boots and laced them up. She grabbed her camera bag, then stopped.

Ella was suddenly overwhelmed with the most powerful feelings of hunger she could ever remember. She felt like she would pass out if she didn't have something to eat. A crust of bread would be a king's feast. But she could do better than that. In her camera bag she found a Snickers candy bar, then an Almond Joy. She ripped the wrapper off the Snickers and shoved it in her mouth. She placed the Almond Joy in her shirt pocket.

Ella started towards the landmark tree on the ridge, then stopped again. The bristlecone pines beyond the horses were perfect, especially with the animals in the foreground to give depth and perspective. She took four or five pictures of the trees, grabbed two donuts out of the grub bag, then resumed her journey to the top of the hill.

When she reached the tree, she could see Emmett a short distance beyond, kneeling behind a big rock, looking out onto the table with his binoculars. Beyond him in the distance were five or six deer. She crept up to Emmett and knelt beside him, leaning her head on his shoulder.

"What is wrong with their horns?" she asked. "Why are they so thick, and sticking out to the side like that?"

"Antlers, not horns," he said. "The bucks grow new ones every summer. They are covered with velvet while they are growing. That's why they look thick. On mature bucks the antlers grow out from the skull, then up. This early in the season the antlers haven't started to grow up yet. That's why they look funny or different to you." He started to hand Ella the glasses, but she had already attached her telephoto lens and was beginning to take pictures.

When she was finished they hurried across the table to the cliffs Emmett had told her about. When she saw them—sheer, black walls of wet rock, falling many hundreds of feet down into dark forests—she couldn't help but wonder what it would have been like wandering off the edge during the blackness of the night.

When she finished photographing the cliffs, she got some closeups of little clumps of yellow and purple flowers, some landscape shots of Mt. Moriah with a golden eagle soaring in the foreground, and a few long-range shots of a bighorn sheep. When she was finished, Ella had used up four rolls of film. She gave half of her Almond Joy to Emmett as they started back to camp, hand in hand.

"What happens now?" she asked.

"I'll cook up an old-fashioned, unhealthy country breakfast," he said.

"I mean, between us, after last night."

"I want you to know I didn't plan anything," he said. "I really was concerned about your hypothermia, and didn't know what else to do."

"As far as I am concerned you saved my life, twice in one night, and you have nothing to apologize for. What happened after the hypothermia is probably more my fault than yours, anyway."

"That I concede," he said.

"You can't get off that easy," Ella teased. "Remember, you are the one who crawled into my sleeping bag."

"Yes. And I will never forget it. I've been puzzling over a scripture all morning. I don't even know where it is."

"A scripture?"

"Yes, the one that says something about wickedness never being happiness. If what we did was wicked, I'm not sure I understand the meaning of that verse anymore."

"Maybe our happiness won't last," she offered.

"It can if you marry me," he said.

"Do you want me to load the kids in the back of the Jeep and move out to the ranch with you?" she asked.

"Yes. But along with George, you'd have to give up your teaching career. Would you miss Spanish Fork?"

"It's a good place to raise children," she admitted,

"but it lacks some things as far as adults are concerned. I won't miss it."

"I've thought of selling off some of the cattle," he said, "so I can start writing some of the books we've talked about. Maybe we could work together. The proceeds from the cattle would finance us for a few years."

"I might be able to get a job at the school," she said. "Maybe BYU will fire me anyway when they find out what we did up here."

"Do they have to find out?" he asked.

"It would be nice if they didn't," Ella said. "But we committed adultery. You're not a member, so I guess you get off easy. But if I want to be forgiven, I must confess. I guess I'll have to deal with it when I get home. Let's don't let it ruin today."

"Then you will divorce George and marry me?" Emmett asked.

Ella didn't answer immediately, but turned to face him, without letting go of his hand. They looked into each other's eyes a long time. Gently she kissed him on the lips.

"Yes," Ella finally said. "I will do it."

"You don't have to worry about polygamy. That's over," he said.

"Just promise me one thing," Ella said.

"What?"

"If you do decide to try polygamy again, let me pick the second wife."

"That's a promise. Do you have someone in mind?"

"Yes. Her name is Harriet. I have known her for years. She is a very beautiful person."

"Do I get to meet her first?"

"Absolutely not. I'll just bring her home to dinner some night, and say, 'Emmett, here's your new wife.' Introductions can come later."

"You make it very enticing," he said. "But I think I'll pass. I miss those hymns. I want to get back in the Church. You can help me. If you confess and get excommunicated,

168

maybe we can work our way back together.''

''Doesn't sound like a lot of fun, but we'll be able to do it. What if I'm pregnant? Will that change anything?''

''I guess we'll cross that bridge when we get to it,'' Emmett said.

''Then back to my first question,'' Ella continued. ''What do we do now?''

''Monday morning I'll call the *Western Livestock Journal* and place an ad to sell some of the cattle. Monday morning, you'll call a divorce lawyer and set up an appointment. Monday night we'll touch bases on the phone to see how things went, and determine the next step.''

''You make it sound so simple.''

''Just one step at a time. That's all we can do.''

They were back at camp now. The horses had stopped grazing, and were dozing in the morning sun. The wind was still calm, and the cloudless sky promised a beautiful day. The fire had gone out, so Emmett broke up some sticks to get it going again.

''Before you start fixing breakfast, there's one thing I want you to do,'' Ella said.

''What's that, my love?''

''Do you really love me?'' she asked.

''With all my heart.''

''Then take the tent down before you start cooking breakfast.''

''What?''

''Take the tent down. After what happened last night, and the feelings expressed this morning ... I mean anything could happen while we're fooling around with breakfast, and I don't want to have to render two confessions to the bishop.''

Emmett stopped what he was doing, took Ella in his arms and kissed her again. She wrapped her leg around his as she had done the night before, and kissed him back.

169

Chapter 16

When Ella called Emmett the next Monday night, he reported that he had placed an advertisement to sell some of his cattle in the *Western Livestock Journal.*

She reported that she had called an attorney and set up an appointment for the coming Friday afternoon, the earliest time he could see her.

"Great," Emmett said. "We're putting together a benefit roping next Saturday to buy a nice headstone for Billy Thunder. Lots of ropers coming. We could use your help."

"I'll be there," she said.

"Good.'

"What about the children?" she asked, changing the subject.

"What do you mean?"

"Should I tell them now, or after I file? Should I talk to each one alone, or both of them together? What do I tell them? Should they know about you?"

"I have no experience at this kind of thing," he said.

"If you have a friend who's been through it, maybe she can help. I don't know what to say except that I love you, and know it can all be worked out. Are you getting cold feet?"

"It's going to be harder than I thought," Ella said. "It's almost like George senses something. He's being too nice. He even brought home a football from the office and played catch with Kevin."

"What about the bishop, and your confession?"

"I've decided to wait until the divorce thing is under control. I can't do everything, not at the same time."

"Things will only get better."

"I'm not sure, Emmett. I can't sleep at night. I didn't know it was possible to worry so much. I have no appetite."

"Do you want to call the whole thing off?" he asked.

"Sometimes I feel like doing that."

"Too bad George isn't a wife beater," Emmett said. "That would make it a lot easier."

"Look, I've got cattle buyers coming from Salina and Twin Falls. I'll be hard to reach the next few days. If we don't talk before Saturday, I'll call you after the roping, at nine o'clock. Everyone should be gone by then. I love you, and I'm putting a letter to you in the mail tomorrow. Goodby."

Talking to Emmett made Ella feel a little better, but it was still going to be a hard week. She decided not to say anything to the children until after she talked to the lawyer. He would probably be able to tell her what to do. In fact, he should be able to answer almost all her questions. Ella pulled a yellow notepad out of the drawer and began making a list of questions.

When she had filled three pages, Ella swallowed two sleeping pills, turned off the light and tried to go to sleep. George was not in the bed, but upstairs watching a replay of one of the many important big games. She could smell the popcorn, and assumed he had mixed up a pitcher of Kool-Aid too.

Ella didn't know if George was watching a football or

Chapter 16

basketball replay, only that Jay Monson was the announcer. Behind the closed door she couldn't recognize the words, only the sound of the voice. She was not annoyed. Monson's voice was a common fixture around the house, like the sound of the refrigerator motor going on and off. She wasn't sure if it was the soothing voice or the pills that finally put her to sleep.

On Thursday Ella received Emmett's letter. He brought her up to date on the events at the ranch and the upcoming roping. He regretted not being able to help her more with the divorce, and included a quotation from his favorite author, M. Scott Peck, to explain how he felt:

The ultimate goal of life remains the spiritual growth of the individual, the solitary journey to peaks that can be climbed only alone.

Significant journeys cannot be accomplished without the nurture provided by a successful marriage ... It is the separateness of the partners that enriches the union. Great marriages cannot be constructed by individuals who are terrified by their basic aloneness ... Genuine love not only respects the individuality of the other but actually seeks to cultivate it, even at the risk of separation or loss.

On Friday, not only did the lawyer answer most of Ella's questions, but he gave her two or three yellow notepad pages of new questions to think about—items having to do with dividing assets, child custody, child support, and the alimony she might have to pay because she earned more than George. He told her there was a good chance she would have to hire a family therapist to help the children adjust to the divorce.

When she told the lawyer how she was leaving dependable George for a cowboy who used to be a polygamist, the attorney only scratched his head and gave her a blank stare. The session ended with a detailed explanation of the attorney's fee schedule. When she handed him a check for $500 she had the feeling this was just the first of many

173

such checks.

Ella left the office with one unanswered question. Why did so many people get divorced? It appeared so hard, so stressful, so expensive. She decided there were probably a lot of people who stayed in marriages a lot worse than hers. Good old George didn't deserve a divorce, just because he loved football, popcorn and Kool-Aid more than his wife. She decided to tell George what she was doing as soon as he came home from work. Afterwards, she would tell the children.

When she arrived home Kevin was in the front yard practicing batting with a friend. The previous evening, Kevin had been allowed to start at second base on his Pony League team, the first time Kevin had started on a team since Little League. Kevin had hit a double his first time at bat, and later in the game, a single. Ella wondered how Kevin would respond when she told him she was moving him to the West Desert where they didn't have organized baseball for boys his age. He would probably be angry.

When she greeted the boys, Kevin asked if he could have dinner with his friend. She said he could.

A few minutes later, Ella found Laura in her room, crying. Laura's boyfriend, Brett, had asked another girl to the school dance. Laura wanted to know why the Mormon Church didn't have a program like the Catholics that allowed women to become nuns. Ella offered some comforting words, assuring Laura that she was a beautiful young woman, and boys better than Brett would come into her life.

As Ella left the room, she realized how immature and potentially vulnerable her daughter was. What were the risks of taking a beautiful young woman like Laura to a community abounding with polygamists?

Ella pondered this question and a hundred others as she prepared the evening meal, consisting of meat loaf, baked potatoes, and peas.

When George came home, he was visibly upset. When dinner was served, it was just Ella and George at the table. Laura was still in her room, insisting she was not hungry.

Chapter 16

George explained how the dean had asked him if he would be willing to work in physical facilities instead of athletics.

"They want to take me out of football and make me a janitor," he moaned.

"Will they reduce your pay?" she asked.

"No."

"You can still go to the games."

"It won't be the same," he said.

"No, it won't," she agreed. "Do you want to quit?"

"Yes," he said, thoughtfully, "but I probably won't. I guess I'll be their janitor."

They ate the rest of the meal in silence, Ella deciding to talk to the bishop about asking George to coach one of the young men's basketball teams the coming winter. Then she tried to figure the best way to tell George she was going to divorce him. But she couldn't do it. It seemed so cruel to throw another burden on his already crushed ego.

After dinner George made up a double batch of popcorn, a pitcher of blue Kool-Aid, went upstairs, and shoved a video in the VCR. Instead of a BYU football or basketball game, it was the Kevin Costner movie, *Dances With Wolves*.

When Ella finished cleaning the kitchen, she went into the bedroom, shut the door, and called Emmett.

"I can't do it," she said when he picked up the phone.

"Things didn't go well with the lawyer?" he asked.

"It's not that," she said. "It's my family. I can't get over the feeling that this divorce is a mean, rotten thing to do to them. I feel selfish. I was going to tell George at dinner, but I couldn't do it. I can't do it tonight, and I don't think I will be able to do it tomorrow."

"Then it's over?" Emmett asked.

"I don't know what else to do," she sobbed. "I don't want an affair."

"It wasn't just chance that brought us together," he said. "We can't turn our backs on destiny."

"I don't know what else to do," she cried.

175

"Then you're not coming to the roping?"

"No. I couldn't handle that."

"You never want to see me again?" he asked.

"I didn't say that," she moaned, her chest so full of emotion that she could hardly talk. She wanted to get off the phone.

"I'm going to hang up," she sobbed.

"I'm going to call you tomorrow, after the roping. Promise me you'll be there, that you'll talk to me," he pleaded. "I'll call at nine."

"I'll be here," she said, hanging up the phone.

At nine o'clock the next evening Ella was sitting in bed, trying to read, the phone close by. George was doing some public relations at the grand opening of a sporting goods store. The children were at a church dance. Ella was not looking forward to the conversation with Emmett. Though she longed to hear his voice, nothing had changed since the previous evening. The divorce still looked like an insurmountable barrier between her and Emmett.

At nine-fifteen she put the book down. She couldn't concentrate. Emmett had always been so responsible, so punctual. Maybe he had decided not to call. Maybe she would never hear his voice again.

At nine-thirty Ella got out of bed and started pacing. He couldn't have forgotten. Maybe some of his cows had gotten into someone's hay field. Maybe there had been an accident or fire in the valley and he had gone to help. Maybe one of the ropers had driven over the telephone pedestal by the front gate and the phone wasn't working. She dialed his number, and could hear the phone ringing, but no one answered.

At ten o'clock she took a sleeping pill, not two, in the event he still tried to call her. Ella turned off the light and pulled the covers up to her chin. The thought that Emmett might never call gave her a momentary feeling of relief, quickly followed by the most empty feeling she had ever experienced—a feeling of emptiness that only Emmett could fill. She longed to hear his voice, feel his touch. She longed for the entertaining conversation and more nights in the blue sleeping bag.

At ten-thirty the phone rang. She snapped it up. "Hello."

"Is this Ella?" said a male voice. It was not Emmett, but the voice was remotely familiar.

"Who is this?" she barked, almost rudely.

"Wade. Wade Hanks, the roper."

"I'm sorry I was sharp with you. Emmett was supposed to call at nine. I've been worried."

There was silence on the other end of the line. Then Ella could hear Wade blowing his nose.

"What's wrong? Is Emmett hurt?" she demanded, unable to bear the silence any longer.

"Worse than that," Wade said, between sniffs. "We headed and heeled a steer in pretty good time." She wanted to scream at him to get to the point, but talking was better than silence. Anything was better than silence. So she let him continue, between sniffs.

"When the run was over, the steer didn't want to go down to the stripping chute, so Emmett rode alongside to take off his head rope. As Emmett was bending down to get his rope, I thought I'd have a little fun, so I slapped the steer on the butt, thinking it would run away. Instead it jumped towards Emmett's horse, bumping the horse with the left horn. The horse lunged sideways while Emmett was bending over. He lost his balance, and on the way down caught his foot in the stirrup.

"Somebody left the arena gate open. The horse ran down the road, all of us chasing it, our ropes swinging. It jumped the first cattle guard. We had to stop and open the gate. By the time we caught up, Emmett was in pretty bad shape, but still alive. I just cut the stirrup off with my knife.

"We called 911 and they sent out the helicopter from Wendover. It brought him and me here."

"Where?" she managed to gasp.

"The medical center in Provo. He died on the way."

Ella felt numb, like her heart had been ripped out of her chest. She almost dropped the phone. There was a sharp pain in her stomach, her chest, her head. She felt herself slipping into a less painful past, a place of a thousand thoughts and memories. Deer running in front of her Jeep. Emmett riding into her life on a horse named Geronimo. Taking the deer to the hermit. Riding horseback through Emmett's healing place, the site of the Goshute massacre. The first meal together, wild rice stir fry and trout, a warm spring breeze, Emmett's lecture on laziness. Her anger when she discovered his fuel tanks were not empty. The conversations with Harriet as the mystery of Emmett Hays gradually unfolded. An exciting day at the ranch roping, followed by an evening on the mountain with the mustangs. The night on the hill, following the lecture to the breeding bulls. But most of all the trip to Moriah, getting lost in the storm, the gunshots, the pinpoint of light, falling gloriously happy into Emmett's arms. The hypothermia, feeling herself slip into a cold, black grave, and the warmth from Emmett's body bringing her back, turning her icy sleeping bag into a place too wonderful for words to describe.

"Hello, hello ..." She had forgotten she was in a telephone conversation with Wade. As she forced herself to respond, the sharp pains returned.

"Did he say anything before he died?" Ella asked.

"Yes. He was worried about not being able to call you on time. Asked me to do it. Told me your phone number. I wrote it down."

"Why did you wait so long?"

"Because I had to screw around. One life is ended, and maybe another ruined. I needed a few beers to get the courage up to call."

"Did he say anything else?"

"He said he would sell his ranch a thousand times if he could spend one more minute with Ella."

"Anything else?"

Chapter 16

"No."

"I need your help," she said, suddenly feeling cold and strangely in control. "Can you get a truck or van?"

"Got some roping buddies in Spanish Fork. They'll give me a truck."

"We've got to take Emmett back to Pleasant Valley," she said, gradually getting control of herself. "He wanted to be buried on the hill above the arena."

"You can't bury people on the open range anymore," Wade said. "It's against the law."

"Are they going to fine Emmett, or put him in jail?"

"Good point. Get your pants on, lady. I'll pick you up in about an hour. What's your address?" As soon as she told him, Wade hung up the phone.

An hour later she was watching the driveway from the front window. George and the children had come home and gone to bed. She had thrown a pick and shovel on the front lawn, intending to take them along. She was wearing the red and black wool shirt Emmett had given her, and a jacket.

Wade was on time. As soon as she saw the truck slowing down, she headed out the door, picking up the shovel and pick as she crossed the lawn.

Wade was driving a white Dodge pickup. Carefully, she looked into the box. It contained a black body bag.

"Are you sure it's him?" she asked, her stomach suddenly knotted in pain. She wanted to scream, and never stop.

"I unzipped it to make sure," Wade said. "It's him. Don't think you want to look." She placed the tools in the back and climbed in the cab with Wade. She moved like a zombie.

"Did you have any trouble getting the hospital to release him?" she asked.

"Nope. Earlier I'd seen them put him in the refrigerator room, where the mortuary guys come in the morning to get the bodies. There's an outside nearby. Not a lot of lights. Don't think they want the public to see body bags coming out of the hospital, just smiling faces."

"Anyway, I put on one of them green monkey suits and borrowed a clipboard off the bed of an old guy who looked like he was asleep. I just marched in the refrigerator room, started peeking in bags until I found the right one, then wheeled him out the door. My buddies helped put him in the truck. Don't think anybody saw us."

"You stole him," she said.

"How could I steal him from them when they didn't own him in the first place? The way I look at it, I just picked up an old friend who wanted to go home."

They rode in silence for a long time, down the freeway to Nephi, west to Leamington and Lyundyl, past the Intermountain Power Project to Topaz Mountain, then on the dirt road to Trout Creek. It was still dark, but the stars were beginning to fade when they reached the ranch.

Ella told Wade how to drive to the top of the hill by going around to the back side where it wasn't so steep. When he stopped the truck, they were within ten feet of Jennifer's and Mary's graves.

After Ella picked a spot between the two graves, she and Wade started digging. He picked and she shoveled for a while. Then they changed tools. There were a lot of rocks and the digging was difficult, but they persisted until the morning sun was coming over the Confusion Range.

"Maybe we should call everybody and have a funeral service before we dump him in the hole," Wade said.

"I thought of that on the way out," she said. "But if very many people know he is here, maybe the authorities will find out and insist he be moved, and Jennifer and Mary, and little Rebecca with him."

When the hole was almost finished, Ella excused herself, saying she had to get something at the house. Instead of going to the house, she went to the tack room, opened the canvas top pack and removed the blue sleeping bag in which she had been so cold, and then so warm. Taking the bag with her, she returned to the hill where the digging was finished.

180

Chapter 16

"Never heard of anybody ever being buried in a sleeping bag," Wade said as he helped slide the body inside, without removing the body bag.

"This bag was Emmett's favorite place to sleep," Ella said. Wade thought it best not to ask any more questions as they lowered Emmett to his final resting place.

"Shouldn't we say something before we cover him up?" Wade asked.

"I think that would be appropriate," she sobbed. "You go first."

Wade looked at Ella, then at the sleeping bag in the hole. He excused himself for a moment as he returned to the truck and got something from behind the seat. A rope. A brand-new head rope. He hurried back to the grave, removing his black ball cap as he walked.

"Emmett," Wade began, as he gently tossed the rope into the grave. "You know I didn't mean any harm when I slapped that steer on the butt. But shit happens. I'm sorry. I don't know where you are going, but I hope you can rope and tend a few old cows. Amen." He stepped back, waiting for Ella to say her piece.

She stepped forward, biting her upper lip. She opened her mouth, then closed it. For the first time since the accident, she began to cry, great tears falling from her cheeks onto the front of the wool shirt. Sobs of agony squeezed from her throat. Wade put his arm around her, but Ella could not be comforted. Wade stepped away from her, grabbed the shovel, and with the energy of a demon, began pushing the dirt and rock into the hole until it was full.

He turned to Ella. "Would you like to have one of his horses?"

"Not the one that dragged him to death," she sobbed, somehow managing to get the words out.

"That was Geronimo. I'll take care of him."

"Are you going to destroy him?" she asked.

"No. Wasn't the horse's fault he got jabbed in the ribs with a horn. If anything or anybody needs to be destroyed, it's

181

me."

"You can't blame yourself," Ella said. "Had I gone to the roping, I would have kept the gate closed. Maybe I'm to blame."

"Like I told Emmett," Wade said. "I didn't mean any harm."

"Are you going to be all right?" she asked.

"Sure," he said. "I'll bring the filly, the one he called Tithing, over in a few weeks." He gave Ella instructions on where to return the truck.

Wade had decided to stay at the ranch and take care of some of Emmett's last business. His truck and trailer were still there because he had gone to Provo with Emmett in the helicopter.

"Goodby, Wade. Goodby, Emmett," Ella said as she got in the truck to begin her long journey back to Spanish Fork, back to George, back to the Church—but part of her would remain behind in Pleasant Valley near the Moriah wilderness, the healing place and the dying place for Emmett Hays.

The End

Lee Nelson books available by mail

All mail-order books are personally autographed by Lee Nelson

The Storm Testament, 320 pages, $12.95

Wanted by Missouri law for his revenge on mob leader Dick Boggs in 1839, 15-year-old Dan Storm flees to the Rocky Mountains with his friend, Ike, an escaped slave. Dan settles with the Ute Indians where he courts the beautiful Red Leaf. Ike becomes chief of a band of Goshutes in Utah's west desert. All this takes place before the arrival of the Mormon pioneers.

The Storm Testament II, 293 pages, $12.95

In 1845 a beautiful female journalist, disguised as a school teacher, sneaks into the Mormon city of Nauvoo to lure the polygamists out of hiding so the real story on Mormon polygamy can be published to the world. What Caroline Logan doesn't know is that her search for truth will lead her into love, blackmail, Indian raids, buffalo stampedes, and a deadly early winter storm on the Continental Divide in Wyoming.

The Storm Testament III, 268 pages, $12.95

Inspired by business opportunities opened up by the completion of the transcontinental railroad in 1870, Sam Storm and his friend, Lance Claw, attempt to make a quick fortune dealing in firewater and stolen horses. A bizarre chain of events involves Sam and the woman he loves in one of the most ruthless schemes of the 19th Century.

The Storm Testament IV, 278 pages, $12.95

Porter Rockwell recruits Dan Storm in a daring effort to stop U.S. troops from invading Utah in 1857, while the doomed Fancher Company is heading south to Mountain Meadows. A startling chain of events leads Dan and Ike into the middle of the most controversial and explosive episode in Utah history, the Mountain Meadow Massacre.

The Storm Testament V, 335 pages, $12.95

Gunning for U.S. marshals and establishing a sanctuary for pregnant plural wives, Ben Storm declares war on the anti-Mormon forces of the 1880s. The United States Government is determined to bring the Mormon Church to its knees, with polygamy as the central issue. Ben Storm fights back.

Rockwell, 443 pages, $14.95

The true story of the timid farm boy from New York who became the greatest gunfighter in the history of the American West. He drank his whiskey straight, signed his name with an X, and rode the fastest horses, while defending the early Mormon prophets.

Walkara, 353 pages, $14.95

The true story of the young savage from Spanish Fork Canyon who became the greatest horse thief in the history of the American West, the most notorious slave trader on the western half of a continent, the most wanted man in California, and the undisputed ruler over countless bands of Indians and a territory larger than the state of Texas, but his toughest challenge of all was to convince a beautiful Shoshone woman to become his squaw.

Cassidy, 501 pages, $16.95

The story of the Mormon farm boy from Southern Utah who put together the longest string of successful bank and train robberies in the history of the American West. Unlike most cowboy outlaws of his day, Butch Cassidy defended the poor and oppressed, refused to shoot people, and shared his stolen wealth with those in need. Nelson's longest book.

Storm Gold, 276 pages, $14.95

This historical novel focuses on a formerly unknown Indian massacre of hundreds of Spaniards in central Utah, bringing to an abrupt end over 200 years of exploitation by Spanish adventurers and priests. A story of gold, love, passion and war--Nelson story telling at its best.

Favorite Stories, 105 pages, $9.95

A compilation of Lee Nelson's favorite short stories, including Taming the Sasquatch, Abraham Webster's Last Chance, Stronger than Reason, and The Sure Thing.

The Moriah Confession, 182 pages, $14.95